Me and My Girl

Me and My Girl

C. N. Phillips

www.urbanbooks.net

Urban Books, LLC
300 Farmingdale Road, NY-Route 109
Farmingdale, NY 11735

Me and My Girl Copyright © 2018 C. N. Phillips

ISBN 13: 978-1-945855-11-5
ISBN 10: 1-945855-11-8

First Trade Paperback Printing September 2018
Printed in the United States of America

10 9 8 7 6 5 4 3 2 1

*This is a work of fiction. Any references or similarities
to actual events, real people, living or dead, or to real
locales are intended to give the novel a sense of reality.
Any similarity in other names, characters, places, and
incidents is entirely coincidental.*

Distributed by Kensington Publishing Corp.
Submit Orders to:
Customer Service
400 Hahn Road
Westminster, MD 21157-4627
Phone: 1-800-733-3000
Fax: 1-800-659-2436

Me and My Girl

C. N. Phillips

A Message to the Readers

Oh, my goodness! First, I want to say that you all give me life. I just want to thank you from the bottom of my heart for every ounce of the support you have given me over the years. I appreciate you for trusting my mind enough to go out and grab these crazy-ass stories that have jumped out of my head and onto paper. This dream of mine has come so far, but we aren't through yet, believe that! There are so many more worlds to create, so I hope you're ready to explore them with me. You are about to dive headfirst into a spine-tingling thriller that I enjoyed weaving together for you. I hope you're ready for one hell of a ride!

To Carlotta Phillips

Hi, Mommy! I love you with my entire heart, and I really wish you were here because sometimes I really need you. But I know you didn't leave me because you wanted to, and I'm not mad at you for that. I know I used to wonder if you would be proud of me if you were here, but I don't anymore. I know you are because I feel it all around me every day. I don't know who you're whispering to up there, but I know that these blessings are coming from you. I miss you so much, and I can't wait to see you again. But until then, thank you, Mommy. For everything.

Chapter 1

Matise

"I want you to meet someone."

Those were the words that changed my life. Well, maybe not my life, but a big part of it. Jordan Heart had been my best friend for as long as I could remember. It was always Matise and Jordan, Jordan and Matise. He was a nerdy kid back then, complete with the thick glasses and buck teeth. I wasn't much better, being the lengthy, awkward girl with the long ponytail. Not to mention my acne was on fleek. We became friends by chance but stayed friends by choice. As the years went by we grew together and shed our ugly shells. Through our friendship, our parents even became the closest of friends.

The true feelings that I had for Jordan didn't begin to show until our senior year of college. It was getting almost impossible to hide them, especially with as fine of a young man he had grown into. I stood on the sidelines, watching him go through girl after girl since high school, and it had started to take a toll on me. In college, Jordan was what every girl on campus could call a solid catch. He was in school for software development, and since his family owned one of the biggest software companies in Nebraska, he was promised a major job in the company.

I know, you're probably waiting for the part where I tell you about how I confessed my love to him and we lived happily ever after, right? Well, that part doesn't come. I mean, of course I planned to tell him that I was madly in love with him. From the tips of his short, curly hair all the way down to his toes. Wait. Let me rethink that. I hate feet. But you get my point. I actually did try to tell him how I felt the night of our college graduation.

Our parents had come together and planned the most beautiful dinner for us to welcome the next stages of our lives. My father owned an entertainment and media business called Angel Media that was based out of downtown Omaha. He hosted the entire dinner celebration in the banquet hall of the big building and invited everybody he could think of. When I say they went all out? They went all out. Since it was a winter graduation, there were ice sculptures throughout the large hall. The lights were dimmed so that the glittery sparkles projecting on the walls and tables could stand out. Hanging from the crystal chandeliers were pictures of both Jordan and me from babies to adults. Thinking back to that day made the butterflies flutter in my stomach the same way they did back then.

"Matise, darling! You look absolutely stunning!"

"Thank you, Auntie Lisa," I said, smiling at my portly aunt.

She was a sweetheart when she wanted to be. And by "when she wanted to be" I mean when people were watching. She was my mother's older sister, and she reminded her of that whenever she got a chance. Whereas my mother was content being a housewife, my aunt strived to be much more than that. She graduated with her master's in psychology, and whenever she could get the chance, she was always trying to get into someone's head. Aunt Lisa was a thicker woman, who wore her hair in a short, curly afro. She was pretty with a nice-sized bust and bottom, and because of that, she never had a problem getting a man. Now keeping them, that was a different story.

"All that beauty must have taken time. I'm assuming that's why you're late to your own party?"

I had to bite my inner cheek to keep from rolling my eyes and saying something smart back to her. Of course, she just had to be the first person I bumped into upon my slightly late arrival. My mama had always taught me that if I didn't have anything nice to say, don't say anything at all. I offered her the nicest smile I could muster, given the fact that I was still biting my cheek, and I continued past her into the banquet hall.

My parents had truly outdone themselves. I was completely taken away by the decorations. It was like I was in some sort of winter wonderland. I spotted my parents standing next to Jordan's parents near the punch table, so I made my way over toward them. On my way, people seated noticed me and offered their congratulations.

"Matise! You look gorgeous, honey!" Mrs. Heart said the moment she saw me. She grabbed my hands and spread them out to get a better look at my dark blue velvet strapless dress. Draped around my shoulders was a white faux fur that went well with the diamond earrings and choker my father had gifted me with earlier that morning.

"Thank you, Mrs. Heart. You look beautiful yourself," I said, commenting on the ankle-length black gown she wore.

"Oh, this old thing?" she said modestly, but the way Mr. Heart's eyebrows shot up at her comment let me know that the dress was anything but old.

That was one thing about Mrs. Heart that I had loved since I had met her. She knew how to let you have the spotlight, even if that meant toning herself down. It was a trait that Jordan, too, had picked up on. He looked just like her too, light brown skin tone and all. His muscles and height he got from his dad. Mr. Heart towered over us all, including my own father, and he smiled down at me.

"I would ask what took you so long to get here," my mom started, "but given that you look just heavenly right now, I won't chastise you too much. Oh, I'm so proud of you, honey!"

"Thank you, Mama," I said and let her embrace me once Mrs. Heart let go of my hands.

She too looked amazing in the red dress she'd chosen for the night. Whereas my aunt Lisa was more on the plump side, my mother's body was so tight it put women my age to shame. Not only was she in shape, but Larise Jackson had curves for days, and I was shaped just like her. Her smooth caramel skin was an exact replica of mine, and so was her flawless white smile. Her pride exuded from her body, and her grin spoke volumes.

My dad placed a big kiss on my forehead and patted my back. "You may have not been the son I wanted—"

"Honey." My mom cut her eyes at him.

"Let me finish, woman!" he said to her and then turned his attention back to me. "You may not have been the son I wanted, but I know now why we sometimes don't get what we want. You are more than I could ever have asked for in my child, and I love you so much for that."

"Aw, Daddy," I said, blinking away my tears. "You're going to make me cry, and I spent an hour on my makeup!"

"I'm just proud of you, that's all! Don't go crying and getting all raccoon in the eyes!"

Both my mom and Mrs. Heart swatted him at the same time. My dad looked to Mr. Heart with wide eyes and put his hands up.

"Listen, you're on your own. That's three against one. My name is Bennet, and I ain't in it!"

We all laughed. While they continued to chat, I found myself looking around the large crowd in the banquet hall. I was looking for one person in particular, but I didn't find him.

"Is Jordan here?" I asked Mrs. Heart.

"Yes, baby. He tried to wait for you to get here to make his plate, but he was so hungry let him tell it. I think he's upstairs on the balcony. Go ahead and make yourself a plate and join him. This is your party. Enjoy it!"

I did exactly what she said and loaded my plate with fried chicken, greens, macaroni and cheese, and cornbread, although I was positive that it wouldn't get touched with the way the butterflies were going crazy in my stomach. On the drive to the party, I had given myself a pep talk about going for what I wanted. I had already obtained my degree in design, and now it was time to get the other thing I wanted: Jordan Heart. Not only was he my best friend, but he was the man I was madly in love with. Except, he didn't know I loved him, in that way at least. But after that night, he would. I couldn't go another day without knowing what his kisses felt like or seeing him look at me the way I dreamed he would one day. I knew that if I didn't do it now, somebody else would beat me to the punch.

"Please be alone. Please be alone. Pleeease be alone," I quietly wished as I made my way up the winding staircase toward the back of the hall.

When I reached the top, I sighed with relief when I saw Jordan sitting by himself by a fireplace, going to town on a piece of chicken. He was so fixated with his food that he didn't even hear me approach until I placed my plate on the table. When he looked up and saw me, he smiled big, the way I hoped he would when he saw me.

"You changed your dress?"

"You noticed," I said, smoothing my hands down my hips. I'd changed from the plain black one I wore to the graduation earlier, wanting to make a lasting impression, hopefully.

"You look good, Te Te."

"Thank you." I smiled shyly at him.

"You're welcome," he said, grinning. *"You must have wanted to match me."*

He flashed the cuff links of his royal blue suit and looked down at himself smugly. I couldn't hold it in. I cracked up. He was so silly I couldn't stand it. He laughed too, showcasing the deep dimples in his cheeks.

My God he's looks so good, I thought, taking in his appearance. It was like my attraction to him was growing by the minute. His hair was neatly lined up and cut into a tapered fade. He had a small mustache and goatee, giving his baby face the look of a grown man. His full lips looked so soft. I wondered what they would feel like on mine, both sets. My feelings for Jordan had grown into sexual desires, and I would have loved to know how it would feel with him between my legs while I looked into his sweet face as we made love. Or what it would be like to—

"It's scary, huh?" he asked, snapping me out of my own head.

"What's scary?" I asked and watched him avert his eyes to the flickering flames that were keeping us warm.

"We crossed over. We're in the real world now."

"It shouldn't be so scary for you. You already have a job, and you haven't even applied yet!"

"Yeah, I guess you're right. But . . ." He let his voice trail off.

"But what?"

"Everybody keeps telling me how lucky I am to be able to work for my old man's company, and in a way they're right. I'm blessed. But he's starting me as a VP. Me, a VP right out of college."

"Whoa."

"Yeah." He shook his head with his brow furrowed slightly. *"He opened the position up just for me. It's just so much pressure to walk in the shoes of a man so great, and I don't know if I will live up to his expectations."*

"You don't have anything to worry about."

"And how do you know that?"

My body acted before my brain even told it what to do. My hands reached and grabbed his, forcing him to look back at me. His deep brown eyes were on mine, searching them for an answer.

"Because you have already lived up to his expectations. He wouldn't have given you the job if you hadn't."

"Yeah." He nodded. *"Yeah, maybe you're right."*

"Aren't I always?" I asked.

"So modest," he said sarcastically and shook his head. *"I guess the next step after this would be settling down and putting the player to rest."*

"As if you could do that," I joked just to see what he would say.

"For the right one, I could. I think I just date women for looks. That's why my interest always fades."

"Well duh, I could have told you that!" I said, and we both laughed.

"Okay, since you know so much and since you're the one person in the world who probably knows me like the back of their hand, tell me. What is my perfect girl?"

Here's your chance. *"Well, she's beautiful of course. Funny, but intelligent. She has to sit up all night and not only binge watch every* Star Wars *movie with you, but she has to enjoy them. She has to be laid-back but know* how to have a good time. She must be patient because sometimes it takes a while for you to come off your high horse to admit you're wrong. Of course, she needs to be hardworking and dedicated. And oh, she has to love kids. Your mother has to love her, and she must know how to cook. And lastly, you know how you smile when you're really really happy? She has to make you do that every day without even trying."

"Wow."

I had literally just described myself, and by the way he was staring at me, I thought he had figured it out. I took a deep breath. It was now or never. "Jordan, there is something that I need to talk to you about. It's something that I have been thinking about telling you for a long time. I just didn't know how to."

"Wait." He stopped me and removed his hands from mine. He then reached down and grabbed something from the ground by his feet. "I have something for you."

He handed me a medium-sized gift bag, and a smile instantly came over my face. I was like a kid in the candy shop as I tore into it. When I pulled out a picture album, my heart instantly warmed. On the cover it said, "Best Friends Forever," and inside were pictures of only us, starting from elementary school.

"We weren't even friends when we were this young. How did you get pictures?" I asked in awe.

"Just because we weren't friends doesn't mean our mothers didn't pose us together at birthday parties and school programs."

"True!" I grinned, but his next words took away all of the warmth in my heart.

"Now you're my best friend, Matise. I thank God every day I have someone as solid as you by my side. All these years you have kept me in check, and I'm even more thankful that we have honored our friendship by never crossing lines that can't be erased. Don't get me wrong, you grew from an ugly duckling into a beautiful swan, but I know things between us would never be the same if anything like that were to happen between us. So basically, I'm saying thank you for being my real friend and not treating me like a piece of meat like the rest of these women."

I was sure he expected me to laugh, or maybe tell him to get lost if he ever thought I wanted to sleep with him. But I couldn't. I was too busy willing my tears not to drop and trying to soothe the ache in my heart.

"Matise, are you okay?" he asked.

He was so oblivious to what was happening, I almost laughed. There was no way I could tell him what was really on my mind, so instead, I lied. "Yes, I'm okay. I just never thought you could be so thoughtful, fathead. Thank you," I said.

"You're welcome. There are some pages in the back that don't have pictures in them. I figured we can fill them in with whatever is coming in the future."

"I'm sure we will." I looked up at him when my eyes weren't wet anymore, and I smiled.

"Anyways, what was it that you wanted to tell me?"

"Huh?" I tried to play dumb.

"You said you wanted to tell me something. You pregnant or something?"

"What? No, stupid. I, uhhh . . ." I tried to think fast. "Um, just that I'm moving to New York at the end of the summer. I accepted an interior design job there."

It wasn't entirely a lie. I did have a job offer in New York that I had been seriously considering. The only reason I hadn't accepted it was because I was hoping that Jordan would tell me that he was madly in love with me too and marry me. Okay, maybe I was thinking too much into that, but you get the point. I could have easily found a job in Nebraska, given the connections that my father had, and made that work. However, it looked like that wasn't going to happen.

"New York?" Jordan asked as his face slowly dropped. "That's so far away. There isn't anything here?"

"I mean, I'm sure there is, but for what they're offering me for my starting salary, I couldn't really pass it up."

"So, you'll be living there?"

"Well living here and working there would be a pretty long work commute, so I figured it would be best to move," I answered sarcastically.

"Wow," he said. "Then I guess congratulations. We'll have to make the best of our last summer then."

Last summer. The words lingered in the air like bad breath. That was one thing that I hadn't prepared myself for. "Yeah."

It got quiet. The only thing that could be heard was the crackling of the fire. It warmed my body, but I didn't know if I could say the same about the butterflies in my stomach. It was like they were frozen in place.

"There's only one thing left to say then before we go back inside."

"Yes?" I heard myself ask in a hopeful voice.

"Are you going to eat that piece of chicken?"

The memory faded, and I was glad when it did. I hated to relive that moment, but there I was five years later in my parents' home, staring into the face of the man I still loved as he looked lovingly at somebody else. Somebody else who had a beautiful diamond on her ring finger.

She was a beautiful brown-skinned woman with eyes the same color as mine. The red maxi dress she wore clung to her body very nicely, and her hair hung down to her exposed shoulders. She was smiling in my face, showing off her perfect white teeth, and I wanted to kick my dad for making me be the one to answer the door.

Why had nobody told me that Jordan was bringing some-one with him? I'd spent hours in my old bedroom laying my edges and making sure the ninja bun on the top of my head was perfect. I stood there holding the front door open like a deer caught in headlights with my mouth slightly open.

"Te Te, this is my . . . my fiancée, Lia. Lia, this is my best friend, Matise."

"Te Te, I've heard so much about you!" Lia gushed in this annoyingly cute voice. "I'm so happy to finally meet you."

"Matise," I corrected her. I didn't know her like that. She couldn't call me by my nickname. "And I wish I could say the same. I didn't even know you existed." I turned my attention to Jordan. "Why didn't you tell me that you were getting married? What, did it slip your mind during our daily conversations?"

"Matise, I—"

"Matise, girl, if you don't let that boy and his pretty lady through the door . . . You're letting bugs in my house!" My mom butted in and scooted me out of the way with her soft hands. "Over here hounding this man."

After she moved me, she opened her arms wide and gave Jordan a big hug when he walked through the doorway. I was shocked when she did the same to Lia, and the way she embraced her made me think that it wasn't the first time they'd met.

"Lia!" my father's voice bellowed as he came into the foyer of the house. "I'm so happy that you were able to make it out today. You look stunning. And, my man, Jordan! Your parents are already in the dining room."

"Perfect! I was going to call your mom later, but since she's here I'll see how she feels about me wearing her wedding dress for our wedding!" Lia said.

"That sounds like a lovely idea, dear," my mom said and ushered them away, leaving my father and me alone together.

I didn't know what my facial expression was, but if it showed how I felt inside, then everyone should have been afraid. I was boiling, not only because I hated being left out in the dark, but because they had ambushed me with so much at once.

"So, everyone knew that Jordan is getting married but me?"

"You've just been so busy out of town . . ." My dad's voice trailed off, and I figured it was because he could smell how potent his bullshit was.

"Busy out of town? I talk to Jordan all the time, and not once has he even mentioned Miss Chastity Belt."

"Her name is Lia, and this might be the exact reason why he didn't want you to know. You never approve of anybody he dates."

"Because he has bad taste in women."

"I think you'll like Lia. She reminds me a lot of you."

"Please," I scoffed.

"Be nice," he said and held his arm out. "Let's go back and finish our dinner."

I let him lead me back to the large dining room table, and I purposely avoided eye contact with Jordan. I didn't want to see his fresh haircut or that he was wearing the hell out of his mustard-colored button-up. I sure as hell wasn't trying to see his smile, or his hand on top of hers, so I just sat back down and focused on my ribs, mac and cheese, and baked beans. I didn't really hear much of the conversation going on around me. I tried my best to tune it out and stay out of it. I didn't want to hear how excited Mrs. Heart was when she learned that Lia wanted to wear her dress for the wedding, nor did I want to hear my mother gushing about how beautiful she would be in it.

"So, Te Te, how long will you be in town for?"

I heard Jordan's question, but I didn't bother to look up. *Did that fool really just ask me a question like everything was normal between us? No, he didn't. He couldn't have.*

"Te Te, did you hear me? How long you here for?"

He did. If I could have thrown my entire plate at his face, I would have.

"Monday," I answered as dryly as I could.

"Well, what are your plans?"

"Don't have any," I said to my baked beans.

"Well how about we all do lunch tomorrow? I really want you and Lia to get to know each other."

"Oh! Darn, I forgot I actually have a prior engagement in the afternoon tomorrow."

"Okay, well what about dinner? I know you love that soul-food place on Twenty-fourth. Perfect for Sunday dinner. What do you say?"

"I have something to do then too," I said, that time looking up to glare at him in the eyes. "Honestly, I really don't care to know the girl you've hidden from me for the past six months. It wasn't important then, so it's not important now."

"Matise!" my mother gasped, but I didn't care. I threw my napkin on my barely touched food and pushed away from the table.

"Matise!"

"Leave me alone, Mama," I called over my shoulder.

Everyone was calling out for me. However, I was already halfway to the front door. They must have been out of their minds if they thought I was going to stay under a roof that was holding secrets that hurt me. Tears dropped from the corners of my eyes, not because Jordan had kept his year-long relationship from me, but because after all these years, I had finally lost him for good.

Chapter 2

Matise

"Soooo, how was your trip?"

I knew that question was coming, and that was the main reason I stayed out of my office as much as I could that day. I had gotten back to New York the night before from my visit back home, and I really didn't want to go to work. Then again, I didn't really want to be home and thinking about the fact that my soul mate had found his soul mate and it wasn't me. So, I forced myself to go to work even though my heart was eating itself. I was one of two VPs at Posh Designs, an interior design company that specialized in revamping the insides of current businesses and creating the insides of new ones.

When I first moved to New York, it was a company just getting off the ground, and I was happy to be a part of its growth and development. After the first three years, the company was worth $20 million. Now it was worth $60 million. We even landed a three-year contract with Better Homes television network, showcasing the talents of the company across the world. I was promoted within my first year, and by my third, I had the second largest office in the company, complete with a beautiful view of the city.

My office was a reflection of me, and I viewed myself as a happy person. I decided on a brown cedar desk and yellow traditional high-back chairs. I even had them rip up the old carpet and install a softer brown carpet, mainly because that was my second home, and I often kicked my shoes off while I was at work. My walls were decorated with collage frames with pictures of everyone I held close to my heart, a fifty-inch flat-screen television, and in the corner, there was a grandfather clock just like my grandmother used to have.

I sighed deeply and glanced up at Amara Cane, my assistant and close friend. Remember the show *Girlfriends?* Well, she was the Maya to my Joan, and I loved her dearly. Amara was a beautiful petite chocolate woman with long hair and gorgeous mahogany eyes. She wore her hair with a middle part and pulled back into a neat ponytail with a yellow ribbon that matched the yellow dress she wore. Her head was poked inside of my office, and she had this cheesy smile that caused me to roll my eyes. I should have known she was going to sniff me out sooner or later. I wanted to tell her to mind her business and leave me alone, but I couldn't do that. Especially after expressing to her how excited I was to see Jordan right before I left town.

"Can I come in?" she asked but didn't wait for me to answer. She waltzed right into my office and sat in the comfy chair across from my desk. "Weird. Every other time I came in here to talk to you, you weren't here. Mind you, I've come in here like ten times. It's kind of like you're avoiding me." She raised her perfectly arched eyebrow and looked skeptically at me.

"I've just had a lot of work to do today, that's all."

"Riiight."

"What? I did!"

"So then why is that big pile of papers still on your desk?" She pointed to the paperwork in the far left corner of my desk. "That is the same pile of work that I set there this morning. Come on, Te Te, tell me what's going on with you. Did something happen over the weekend?"

"A lot happened actually," I groaned, realizing that she wasn't going to let me be until I told her.

"Like? I don't understand. You were so excited to go home and see your parents and Jordan. Why the long face? I expected you to be telling me that you finally jumped in bed with your longtime crush."

"Yeah, me too," I said and let out a breath. "When I got there everything was great. You know? My parents were so excited to see me, and my first evening back they had a big dinner for me. They invited the Hearts, and I just knew that would be the time I told Jordan the truth about how I feel. He said had a surprise for me, and apparently, he thought I would be so happy about it, right?" I started to laugh.

"What's funny?"

"He came to my parents' house with another woman."

"What?"

"You heard right."

"He can't do that!"

"Technically, he can. And he did."

"Well she's hideous, right? Like super ugly and bald?"

"Nope." I shrugged my shoulders, killing Amara's hopes. "She's beautiful actually. And she has a head full of hair."

"Okay, but are they serious? I remember you telling me that he's a big player who hates commitments."

"I guess after all these years of playing the field, he is finally ready to give back that player card. They're engaged."

"Engaged?"

"Engaged, girl. The thing that gets me is that they've been dating for six months. As many times as I've been home and as much as we talk, Jordan never mentioned her. Now suddenly, they're getting married."

"Oh, Matise. I'm so sorry." Amara grabbed my hands and squeezed them affectionately.

"Yeah." I nodded. "Yeah, me too."

"What's her name?"

"Future Mrs. Lia Heart."

"Ugh. Matise Heart sounds so much better." She rolled her eyes and shook her head. "I can't believe he would bring her to your parents' house and force you to sit there and watch him be all lovey-dovey with her. I can't imagine how you felt watching them hold hands and do that cute couple talk and kiss and—"

"Thanks, Amara," I cut her off and took my hands back. "Thanks so much. You're making me feel so much better."

"I'm sorry! That was so insensitive of me. I was just saying that it probably broke your heart. So, I guess you never told him how you felt?"

"Nope. After I walked out on dinner I just avoided him the rest of the weekend, you know? I just didn't want to see him, because despite my feelings, we should always be friends first. And friends don't lie to each other, especially for six months. I didn't even say good-bye before I left."

"I understand. Plus, why would you want to sit up with him and his new fiancée when you're the one who wants to ride it like a horse?"

My giggle snuck from between my lips. Granted that wasn't appropriate for my employee to say, but she was more than that. Amara wasn't just my assistant. She had been my very first friend when I touched down in New York City and had become my best friend.

"You get on my nerves."

"You know it's true. So what's the plan?" Her facial expression got all mystical like she was thinking of a master scheme. "Sabotage the wedding like in that one movie with Julia Roberts?"

"Girl, no!"

"Then what are we going to do?"

"*I'm* going to just let it go." I put my hands up when she opened her mouth to protest. "I have to, Amara. He looked happy, genuinely happy. I think it's time to put these feelings that I have to rest. I just want to be there to support him."

"Support him by ignoring him all weekend and leaving without saying good-bye? Great idea."

"You know what?" I rolled up a piece of paper and pretended to hit her. "Don't you have some work to do? Get out of my office."

"You've got it, boss!" she said, laughing and standing up to leave. When she was at the door, she turned to face me. "But on a serious note, I think you're making the right decision, boo. No point in wasting any more of your life on a fantasy what-if. You'll be all right, and if you feel like you won't, you know where to find me."

She winked and then she was gone. Once I was alone, I stared at the pile of papers on my desk before I grabbed them and made myself useful. I tried to keep Jordan off my mind, but it was easier said than done. I couldn't help but wonder what he saw in her, and why he had chosen to propose so soon. Amara's words suddenly snuck into my thoughts. As much as I hated to admit it, she was right. What was the point in holding on to a situation that had never and would never happen? Instead of me being sad about losing him to another woman, I should have been thankful for the friendship that we had. No more what-ifs. It was time that I let that part of my life go and move on.

I finished out the work day in a slightly better mood. I even stayed an extra thirty minutes to send over a new office design to my boss. When I finally made it out of there and was safely inside my silver 2018 Range Rover, I found myself singing along to my R&B playlist.

"'Nine one one zero zero twenty-four!'" I crooned and snapped my fingers along to my favorite LSG jam. "'Baby, it's an emergency. I'm calling 'cause I gotta have some more!'"

I kept hitting repeat on the song when it was over and was still singing it when I pulled into the parking garage of my condo. I parked in my designated spot and grabbed my purse and briefcase before getting out. As I made my way toward the glass doors that led to the elevators, I smiled at Dave, the afternoon and evening garage security guard. I paid good money to stay where I stayed. Shoot, they'd better have some security. He was a muscular white man who looked like he could snap a man's neck with his thumb and little effort. He smiled and gave a small wave back as I passed. He was never really a talker. I went through the doors, and the lights illuminated the white hallway, making it seem even brighter. I watched my reflection grow taller in the elevator doors as I got closer to it. Before I could press the button, there was a ding.

"Howard, stop it, not here!"

There was a petite blonde with a red flowy dress on. She had her leg hiked around the shoulders of a Hispanic man, who was kneeling. It was obvious that he was trying to taste something, and the open doors had ruined that. I tried to hide my smirk, but that just made me smile even wider.

"Is there enough room for me in there?" I asked.

The man shot up to his feet, and he looked sheepishly at me. The woman's face had turned beet red, and she avoided eye contact with me at all costs. I stepped out of the way so that they could bustle by, and I got in the elevator. After I pressed the button to my floor, I was tempted to take off my red Balenciaga pointed-toe pumps. It had indeed been a long day, and I couldn't wait to run hot water in my deep tub and soak for at least an hour.

When I finally reached my floor, I didn't even wait for the doors to open all the way when I stepped off and made my way to my front door. I had just rounded the corner when I looked down into my purse to find my keys. I didn't even notice the person standing outside my condo until I heard his voice.

"You must have picked up some extra time at work."

My head jerked up. When I saw the person's face, my hand flew to my chest, and I took a deep breath. "Dammit, Isaiah! You gave me a fright!"

"I gave you a fright?" A grin spread across his handsome yellow face, and he brought a bouquet of roses from behind his back. "These are for you."

Pause.

See, I know what you're thinking. You're probably wondering who the hell Isaiah was and how he fit into my life, right? I guess the answer to that question is that he didn't. Well, not yet. Isaiah Partners was my longtime lover, who had been hinting a lot recently that he wanted to take things to the next level. It was something that I kept avoiding because I was in love with another man and I knew that it wouldn't be fair to him. However, that was in the past now. Or at least it would be.

"For me?" I returned his smile and took the flowers from him.

"Yeah, this time anyways. I almost gave them to your old-ass neighbor, thinking that she was you when she came around the corner."

"Don't do Mrs. Hubert!" I said with a laugh and smelled the roses. "Thank you, they're lovely."

"You're welcome."

"You want to come in?" I asked, digging my keys out of my purse and unlocking the door.

"Nahhh, I just came up here to give you some flowers and bounce."

"Oh, shut up and get in here!"

He flashed his world-famous grin my way again and shut the door behind him once we were inside. We both took our shoes off at the door before stepping on my stainless carpet. I set my purse and briefcase on the light brown high, wooden four-seater table in my dining room. Isaiah flicked on the lights a little ways away in my spacious living room and plopped down on my light blue furniture and put his feet on the ottoman. I had to admit, he was looking good in his gray work suit and fresh haircut.

"I hadn't planned on cooking tonight, soooo takeout?"

"Sounds good. There's that new Chinese joint around the corner I could call. I think I saw delivery on their window."

"Perfect. You do that, and I'm going to hop in the tub."

"I could get in with you," he said smoothly with a smirk.

I walked through the living room and toward the hallway that led to the bedrooms. "No, I just want to soak alone for a good minute. Plus, you look so comfortable where you're sitting. It's almost like you own the place," I teased.

"I mean, I've been here enough, haven't I? Since you refuse to stay the night at my place."

"We've discussed this, Isaiah," I sighed.

It was true. While I'd been to Isaiah's beautiful four-bedroom home in Manhattan, I always left before the clock hit midnight. He, however, had stayed the night at my home many times. I liked it that way, because I had control there. I could wake him up and put him out with no questions asked, versus at his home, where he would possibly wake me up and charm me into staying. I had enough confusing emotions coursing through me at the time, and I did not want to add another, so the arrangement at hand seemed to work for me. I enjoyed Isaiah's company because that's all he was to me, company. I didn't expect anything from him, and he didn't expect anything from me, or so I thought.

Any other woman would have called me a fool for not grabbing hold of Isaiah's arm and not looking back. But I was not any other woman. Yes, Isaiah was handsome. No, not just handsome. Let me stop lying. The man was gorgeous up and down. He was built like a man who spent a nice chunk of time in the gym, and he had the face of one who graced runways. His sharp jaw structure made his cheekbones go high when he smiled. He had full lips that felt heavenly on both sets of mine, and his eyes were a sandy brown color. Whenever he looked at me, he sent electric volts directly to the place between my thighs. Not only that, but the man had an excellent job. At the age of thirty, he was the youngest senior vice president at NYC Partners, a software company that was trailblazing alongside its competition. I had been jumping through hoops to keep things safe between us even though he was almost perfect. Still, now I was starting to rethink that decision. Horrible right? The only reason I'd be bringing Isaiah up to bat was because Jordan was out of the game, and not because I wanted him to be. But maybe the stars were aligning the way that they were because it was time for something new in my life. Eventually, Isaiah would grow tired of the cat-and-mouse game, and where would that leave me in the end?

"But maybe this weekend we can arrange something," I finished and watched a surprised expression overcome his face.

"You serious?" He stood up, grabbed me, and pulled me down onto the couch with him. "Cinderella isn't going to run out at midnight on me like she always does?"

"Stop it!" I exclaimed, giggling uncontrollably when he began to tickle me. "Yes, I'm serious. So, you have three days to practice putting the toilet seat down!"

"You don't have to worry about falling in with me. You might not even want to leave after spending the weekend."

"Is that right?" I looked into his eyes and licked my lips, recognizing the sensual look on his face. I had to. He was just that fine. Like, fine fine, and it was like I was seeing him for the first time. I knew what he wanted. The question was, should I give it to him? You know what? I had to stop playing with myself. My clit was thumping like the beat from the movie *Jumanji,* and the slit in my pussy lips was slippery. Granted, that bath still sounded amazing, but suddenly so did riding his dick until I quivered. I wanted to see how bad he wanted it and what he would do to get it.

"Yeah, that's right," he said. "But I can show you better than I can tell you."

"All right, you can show me by calling to order the Chinese food while I'm in the tub."

I turned on his lap to plant my feet on the ground, and I tried to stand up, but I felt his grip on me grow a little tighter. My back was to him, and his arms were wrapped around my waist, slowly pulling me into him. I felt his warm breath on the back of my neck, and I bit my lip.

"Can I order it after you bounce on my dick like you did last time?" he whispered in my ear.

Damn, I thought and hissed my tongue.

"Hmm?" he asked, and his strong hands slowly began to hike up my skirt. "Can I put it in right here?"

His erection grew eight inches under my plump bottom, and I felt its thickness between my cheeks. Once my skirt was up high enough, I spread my legs so that I could feel his dick pressed against my throbbing clit.

"No panties? You little nasty girl, you're full of surprises, aren't you?"

"Maybe." I looked back at him before I started to move my hips, sliding my wetness up and down his shaft. His hands moved quickly, removing the articles of clothing from my body. My clit needed pressure, and that's what I gave it when I ground down on his thickness.

"Baby, it's so big," I moaned quietly, admiring him.

"Is it?" he asked, gripping my hips so that he could lift me up slightly. "Tell me again."

Before I could utter another word, he roughly slid into me, awakening every sense in my body and making my back arch into his chest. My legs instantly bent so that I could gain my balance with my knees on the couch cushion, and my hands flew to his hands on my hips for support. My moans filled the air because he didn't let me catch my breath before he started throwing wild stokes up at me.

"Tell me," he said in between the splashy sounds of him going in and out of me.

"It's," I breathed and moaned at the same time, "so big! Oh, yes! Fuck me, baby. I need it. I had such a long day."

I finally caught on to the rhythm of his stroke and matched him. Amara had taught me how to wiggle my butt cheeks while riding, and whenever I did that, Isaiah went crazy. She called it "twerking on the D," and it worked every time. He stopped moving and just let me do my thing on him, which was fine with me. I loved working for my nut, because nobody knew my body better than me. I put it on Isaiah so good each time we fucked, and that was probably the reason why he put up with my shit.

Smack!

"Ahh!" I cried out, feeling the sting on my right butt cheek. "Do it again!"

He obliged, but that time he did it a little harder.

"Yes, baby! Pull my hair!"

"You're so fucking kinky," he said and grabbed a fistful of my hair, yanking my head back so that he could whisper in my ear. "You hear that? You hear what my dick is doing to this pussy? He's making her run for that nut. She's so wet, baby. Thirsty pussy–having ass. Ride this dick. Ride this dick, girl. Ooh, I feel it. Oh shit, I feel you, Te Te!"

Indeed, he did. My body gave tiny jerks as the electrifying feeling coursed through me until it hit my clit all at once. Isaiah knew what to do. He wrapped one arm around my waist and stroked my hair with his other hand and gave me long, deep thrusts. I tried to run because the orgasm I was experiencing was so fierce, but I was a fool to think he would let me. My screams drowned out his grunts, and he pumped into me a few more times before he quickly slid himself out of me to cum on my back. His nut was warm, and I looked back at him with my nose turned up.

"What?" he said, grinning at me as the liquid trickled down my back. "I didn't have a condom on."

"That's what my birth control is for," I said and kissed the tip of his nose. "You're lucky that you're so cute."

"At least I painted your back and not your couch this time. Looks like I have to bathe with you after all."

On the last word, he scooped me up into his arms and kicked his pants down the remainder of his legs, leaving them in the middle of the floor. I was still a little shaken from the good beating he had just put down on me, so I was happy that I didn't have to use my legs. I buried my head into his chest and let him carry me all the way to the master bathroom, all the while thinking that maybe taking our relationship up a notch wasn't such a bad idea.

Chapter 3

Matise

The weekend was slowly approaching, and I was getting a little apprehensive about spending it with Isaiah. I mean there was nothing to be nervous about, right? I mean he was only the man I had been sleeping with for the past six months. I should have been ready and willing to spend a romantic weekend getaway with him, right? With Jordan getting married, there was nothing really to hold me back anymore from going forward with my life, so why not? Isaiah was a good and stable man with a great future ahead of him. He wanted to treat me like a queen. Shoot, he already treated me like a queen. So then why was I so nervous?

Was it because I was afraid that I would fall in love with him and I didn't want to fall in love with him? But why wouldn't I want to fall in love with him when he was all the things that I wanted in my man? From head to toe, Isaiah had it going on, so I was going to at least try to give the thing between us a whirl, even if it killed me.

After the Monday evening and night we'd spent together, we hadn't seen each other or talked much. The whole purpose of that was for us to miss one another so that way the weekend could be even more magical. That was his plan, but for me, not seeing him was just giving me anxiety. I didn't know how it was going to go, and I didn't know how I was going to be. I had never stayed overnight at any man's house. Well, besides Jordan's, but that was different. I just felt that once I dove all the way in with Isaiah, there was no going back. Maybe I was thinking too much into it, but by the time Thursday rolled around I was a complete shipwreck. And, of course, Amara let me know it.

"Girl, Monday you walked in here walking funny, acting happy, and smiling like the sun was out even though it was raining. But now you look like one of them fiends in *New Jack City!* What's going on? I know you're not stressing about spending the weekend with that fine-ass man."

I sighed loudly when she came in to bring me my daily stack of work assignments. I should've known that she was going to come sniffing around and stick her nose all in my business. She had a way of always knowing what was wrong with me even when I didn't say anything about it. I guess that's what made her a great friend. And I had to admit she was right. I was looking a hot mess. I hadn't put on any make-up that morning. All I had done was throw my hair in a ponytail and, honey, I didn't even slick my edges.

"Amara, I don't know if I can do it. I don't think I'm ready yet."

"What do you mean you're not ready? You have been sucking and fucking all over this man for the past six months, and you mean to tell me you can't spend a weekend with him?"

"Okay, but we both know what that was. Booty calls. If I go and I spend the weekend with him, that means we are dating. Like, really dating. And I don't know if I am ready to give my heart to somebody else right now."

"Wait, didn't you say this was your idea?"

"Yes!" I exclaimed. "But I don't think I thought it all the way through. I was just trying to force myself to get over Jordan, but I feel like I'm doing it the wrong way."

"Girl, you know my motto: 'the best way to get over somebody is to get under somebody new.' So, stop being scared, because guess what. If after this weekend you don't feel like you guys can go anywhere, or you don't feel like you're ready for a relationship, it's called communication. Tell him you don't want to do it and that you want to keep things the way they are right now. That's not that hard. But I definitely think that you should go, and you know what else I think?"

"What?"

"I definitely think that you need to put a brush to them edges, girl, because you came to work looking rough. There can only be one unprofessional friend, and sorry, that spot is taken."

"You know what, Amara? I can't stand your ass!" I said, but I still took the brush and small container of gel she carried in her Coach crossbody. "And I'm not even going to ask you why you carry this around with you."

"You can ask if you want to, because I'm sure going to answer! You never know when you need a touch-up. Especially when you're sneaking out of a man's house at eight in the morning!"

"You get on my nerves!" I said, touching my temples with my pointer fingers like she was giving me a headache.

"Girl, stop lying. You love me, and you know I'm the only reason you even want to come to this job every day."

I sighed deeply, and we connected eyes for a few moments.

"I don't even know what we're going to do, girl. Will you come and help me tonight pack some clothes that are appropriate for any occasion?"

"You don't even need to ask me. I already put in my PTO to get off two hours early."

"Amara!" I laughed so hard I couldn't even hold the brush to my head right.

"What? I had plans with my own knight in shining armor tonight, but my sista is more important."

"Who was it, Jacob?"

"Girl, no. I dropped him like he was too heavy. My new thang's name is William, and I've been making him wait for it."

"Whaaaat! Loose-coochie Judy is making somebody wait?"

"See, I'm gon' let that slide since you're going through a crisis and whatnot." Amara cut her eyes and pointed one finger at me. "And yes, I'm trying something new. You know black men always change once they get the goodies."

"Black men? Try all men."

"Well, either way, tonight was supposed to be the night I found out if he gets the nickname Big Dick Willie!"

I finished touching up my hair and double-checked my appearance with the camera of my phone. She gave me the thumbs-up sign, and I figured she was telling me that I looked loads better than before. Handing her back the brush and gel, I shook my head.

"Don't worry about it then, Rah. I don't want to ruin your night just because I'm a total and complete mess."

"Hell no! Trust me, William can wait. This is the first time since I've met you that you've even considered dating somebody seriously. I was always rooting for you and Jordan to one day get together, especially since you were so head over heels. But since that ship has sailed? Honey, we need to get Stella's groove back. You have literally been single your whole adult life, and that is absurd, so I will be there tonight to help you."

"Thanks. I don't know what I would do—"

Ding!

I heard the bell ring letting us both know someone had come up to our floor. Amara's desk was right outside my office, and my office was a room inside of a large suite. I raised my eyebrow at her, and she smiled sheepishly down at me.

"Did you lock the glass doors?"

"If I say no will that make you less mad at me?"

"Rah!"

"I know! I know! I just wanted to have some girl talk without any interruptions. Dang! I'll go see who it is."

"Please do, and don't lock the doors again."

She jetted out of my office, and I quickly pulled up my calendar on one of my double monitors. I checked my schedule, and just like I thought, I didn't have any appointments until later in the afternoon, so I wondered who had shown up. I got my answer within a few seconds when Amara came back into my office with wide eyes.

"Who is it?"

"Uh, umm. Uh—"

"For Christ's sake, Rah!" I stood up and stabbed the floor with my pumps as I made my way to my office door. "Who is i—"

I froze the instant I stepped out of my office. I felt like a kid who forgot her play lines on opening night. There, standing in front of Amara's desk, was the one person I would last expect.

"Hi!" Lia said when she saw me.

She was wearing a pretty blue pencil skirt with a light pink low-cut blouse. Her hair was pulled back into a ponytail, like mine, and she had this huge smile on her face like she was happy to see me. What the hell was she doing there? And how did she know where to find me?

"H . . . hi," I said and furrowed my brow in confusion. "Lia? What are you doing here?"

"I just figured that it might be your lunchtime and we could grab a bite to eat."

"Umm . . ."

"I know this might seem a little weird, me being here."

"Umm . . ." I lifted my brows and shifted my eyes from her to Amara and then back to her. "A lot weird actually. I didn't know you were coming."

"I know! If you did, you probably wouldn't be at work, or anywhere else that I could possibly find you."

"You're right. So why are you here exactly?"

"Jordan was really upset at the way you stormed out of dinner and the way you avoided us the whole time you were home. I know you have a right to be upset, but I just don't want you guys to be at odds because of me. He told me you haven't been answering any of his phone calls or returning any of his voicemails."

"That's right. But I don't see how that's any of your business."

"It's not, but it is. You see, when Jordan isn't happy, I'm not happy. So, I decided to come here to fix it!"

"To fix it?" My voice dropped. I couldn't for the life of me understand what she could possibly think she could fix between Jordan and me, especially when she hadn't known him for even a fragment of the time that I had. And the fact that she had walked in my office looking like she had just stepped out of a photo shoot didn't make matters any better. I couldn't help but glance quickly down at my plain work pants and blazer. I didn't know who she thought she was, but I was about to kick her right on out of my workplace.

"Thanks." I offered her a fake smile back. "But no thanks. I will talk to Jordan when I'm good and ready."

"Are you saying you aren't going to come to the wedding?"

"Ehh, I actually haven't thought that far ahead yet."

"Far?" Lia looked at me with a surprised expression. "The wedding is a month away."

"A month?"

"Yes, we've been engaged for three months already."

"Wow," I said and shook my head. "You guys have . . . my congratulations."

"Do we really? Because the way you left and the way you're so standoffish with me right now are telling me otherwise."

I punched her in her pretty little face. Well, not in real life. But I sure did in my mind. Who the hell did she think she was to tell me how I felt? So what if she was right? She didn't know me like that.

"I'm sorry," she said quickly. She must have felt my vibe, because ooh-wee, I was about to curse her out. "That was out of line. I honestly can't tell you what I would do if I were in your shoes. But please, come to lunch with me? I don't leave until the morning, and I don't know a soul in New York City."

I gritted my teeth and took a big breath. *No matter how you feel about it, she is the girl your best friend is marrying. You're going to have to deal with her sooner or later. Plus, she leaves in the morning.*

I sighed again, that time with a slight eye roll. "Let me grab my purse."

"Yay!" she cheered. "I saw this little joint up the street when I was in the Uber. I couldn't tell if it was Mexican or Chinese though. Or do you want to do upscale? I could sure do a glass of wine!" She spoke with a Southern accent, and she added an extra zing to the word "wine."

Amara followed me back into my office and began whispering frantically at me. "You're about to just go out to eat with her?" She cocked her head and looked curiously at me. "You aren't plotting to kill her, are you? Because if you are, and you need me to help hide the body, you're gon' have to call me on my other phone. That can't lead back to me!"

"Amara, shut up, please. I'm going because I have to. They're getting married, and there is nothing that I can do about it. So I have to deal."

"Okay, but nobody told her to just show up here uninvited."

"I know, but she did. Can you do me a favor and take all of my calls?"

"Of course."

I had no clue what I was getting myself into by agreeing to go to lunch with Lia, but her smile seemed strangely genuine. When we got to the front of my job, there was a black Ford Focus parked and seemingly waiting for us. She walked right up to it and motioned for me to get in when she opened the back door. I slid in, and she did the same.

"I swear, Ubers are probably the best thing known to man!" she said and placed her Louis Vuitton tote bag on her lap.

"Mm-hmm," I said and glanced at the driver. He was a young black guy with a white shirt and a blue snap-back hat on his head. He was my type of driver, quiet and to himself. I hated when they tried to have a conversation with me, but obviously, Lia didn't get the memo.

"So, what's your name?"

"Terry," he said and smiled at her through the rearview mirror.

"Well, nice to meet you, Terry. Have you been an Uber driver for very long?"

"Nah. I actually just started not too long ago. I moved down here to go to school. I start in the fall."

"Nice! Where are you from originally?"

"Massachusetts."

"Massachusetts! Wow, that's different. I'm actually not from here either."

"I can tell by the accent," he said and grinned back at her. "What brings you to the city then?"

"I'm actually here visiting my future sister-in-law."

I almost choked on my spit, and I shot her a look that said, "No, you didn't."

"I'm actually the best friend of her fiancé. I barely know her, and she didn't even tell me that she was coming," I said and glanced back out of the window.

There was an awkward silence, but I wasn't complaining. Anything to stop their annoying small talk. It wasn't until he pulled up outside of a bar that I realized we had gone way past the restaurant Lia originally said we were going to. I raised my eyebrow when I saw that we were parked outside of a small bar called Kenny's. I had gone there a few times with Amara, and it was a nice little spot, but why were we there on my lunch break?

"I thought we were going to get some food," I said when she opened the car door.

"We are." She gave me a mischievous smile. "But we're going to get a drink, too."

"I still have to go back to work," I said like Amara and I didn't drink on our lunch breaks multiple times a week. Still, she didn't know that. "I don't think that would be a good idea."

"Come onnn," she urged. "One drink isn't going to do anything but give you a harmless buzz. Plus, you're already here. Terry, tell her to let loose! Back me up."

"Go have some fun, baby girl," he chimed in, turning around to face me. "Y'all look like you deserve to let loose a little bit."

I didn't know why she thought the words of a someone I had only known for fifteen minutes were going to sway me. I gave him a look like he had bugs on his face before turning my attention back to her. She had this annoying hopeful look on her face, and she held her hand out to me.

"Pleeease?"

"All right," I groaned after a few more moments. "Come on."

I completely ignored her hand and got out on my own side. One drink wouldn't kill me, and with the day I was having, I needed something for my nerves. We entered the dimly lit bar and headed straight to the bar. I ordered a martini, and I didn't really care to hear what she got.

"So be honest."

"About?" I asked, glancing at her on my right.

"What is it about me that you don't like?"

"What gives you the idea that I don't like you?"

"The sarcasm dripping from your voice for one," she sighed. "Is it that you think I'm going to take your best friend away from you?"

"Okay," I said and put my hands up in a "surrender" fashion. "I thought that I could do this, but I can't. Listen, I'm sure you're a great girl and all, but if you came here expecting to leave with my blessing, it's not going to happen."

"But why?"

"Who in their right mind gets married after six months?"

"People who are in love."

"Yeah," I scoffed. "You don't even know each other."

"I do know him!"

"Okay, then. What's his favorite TV show?"

"*Law & Order!*"

"Wrong. *Supernatural.* What does he prefer to dip his steak in?"

"A.1."

"Wrong. Barbecue sauce. What's his favorite drink of all time? I mean, the boy would come running if he knows you have some in your fridge."

"I . . . I don't know."

"Blue Kool-Aid. These are all things that you should have found out in the first month of dating. I didn't even ask you anything hard yet."

"Listen, I don't care what you think. I know that I love him," Lia said, and I could hear the terseness dripping from her tongue.

"Or you love his money."

"What?"

"Come on, Lia. It's no secret that Mr. Heart is planning on retiring soon, which means that Jordan is next in line to run the company."

I paused because by that time our drinks had made their way to us, and I needed something for my nerves to keep me from ripping Lia's head off. As soon as the bartender placed my drink in front of me, I plucked the straw out and threw it to the side. It took all of four seconds for me to completely down my drink.

"You know what gets me? I have seen Jordan go through woman after woman, but none have gotten close enough to get a ring. What did you do, blackmail him?"

"What? I . . . No!"

"Ohh, then he must be pussy whipped. You may have fooled him, but you aren't going to fool me. You women are all the same. You see, you're after one thing, and that one thing isn't his heart. I don't know if you came down here to get my blessing for your little scheme, but it's not coming. Now I've worked very hard to solidify my position in the company I work for. Don't come to it uninvited ever again. Understand?"

I pulled out a twenty-dollar bill and placed it on the bar before getting to my feet and heading for the door. Before I was all the way there, I turned back around to face her distraught expression.

"You know why you can't have my blessing?"

"Enlighten me."

"Because sooner or later Jordan is going to see past that pretty face. He always does."

I left without another word, making a mental note to call Jordan and curse him out from there to the Philippines.

Chapter 4

Matise

As it was, I didn't have to call Jordan and curse him out. He called me. Friday had finally come, and I was making my last preparations for my weekend with Isaiah. All my bags were packed. I doubted that I would need everything in them, but Amara insisted on bringing it all. Isaiah told me that he would be picking me up at noon and to be ready. At exactly eleven forty-five my phone rang, and I answered without looking at the caller ID.

"Hey, baby, are you here yet?"

"Baby? What?"

"Hello? Jordan?" I asked and looked at the phone. Sure enough, it read his contact information. "What do you want?"

"I want to know why you've been avoiding me."

"I mean, you basically lied to me for six months. What do you mean?"

"I didn't lie to you, Matise."

"Keeping secrets is the same thing."

"I didn't tell you because I knew you would react like this."

"I'm reacting this way only because you felt the need to keep a secret from me. And it's obvious that I'm the only person who was kept in the dark. Speaking of Lana—"

"Lia!"

"I don't give a damn what her name is. Tell her not to pop up at my job ever again. What the hell kind of stuff is that?"

"She was just trying to help the situation. She felt like she's the reason why you and I haven't been talking."

"Well, she's wrong about that. You're the reason why we haven't been talking. Secret-keeping ass."

"Can you stop saying that!"

"I will when it isn't true anymore."

"You know what? You are truly something else. And the way you treated Lia when she had nothing but good intentions is ridiculous. She wasn't just there to make things right between you and me. She wanted you to be a part of our day. She was going to ask you to decorate our wedding, because we don't want anyone else to do it. And it would have meant something to me if you did. What kind of person are you?"

"Not the kind that gets married in six months. Are you desperate or something? Did you fall and bump your head? You two don't even know each other."

"Yes, we do!"

"Jordan, she doesn't even know your favorite drink. Y'all don't know each other."

"You always do this when I get into a relationship, Matise. That's why I didn't tell you. You run people off. This is the first time when I have been able to be consistently really happy with someone. So, if you can't accept Lia, then I don't know what to tell you, because she isn't going anywhere."

"Nowhere but in your wallet," I spat back. "And I have never run off anyone you dated!"

"Kim."

"She was a ho! She slept with half the basketball team in college!"

"Tyra."

"She had two kids, Jordan."

"Meghan."

"No woman should feel comfortable with not shaving for months the way she was, okay? That was a big red flag! As a woman, I found that weird."

"See! You aren't my mother, Matise. You act like a jealous girlfriend!"

"Well, I was never that, was I? You just always wanted me as your best friend and that's it."

The moment the words were out of my mouth, I wished that I could take them back. The pause that resonated was an awkward one, and the only thing that could be heard was our breathing. Jordan finally cleared his throat.

"What do you mean by that?"

"Nothing. Nothing at all. But listen, Jordan. You guys can hang up the idea of me decorating your wedding, because I won't even be in attendance. Now if you'll excuse me, my boyfriend will be here any minute to pick me up for our romantic weekend getaway."

Okay, I laid it on thick, but oh well. Forget him and his pretty fiancée. I hung up the phone and tossed it into my purse, ignoring the fact that it started ringing again almost immediately. I knew that it was nobody but him calling me back. However, I didn't want to talk anymore. We had finally reached our crossroads, and it was burning me up inside. I loved Jordan, but it was time to let him go.

I was glad when I finally heard the knock on my door, mainly because it rescued me from being a prisoner of my own thoughts. This was supposed to be a weekend of new beginnings for me, and I wasn't going to ruin things before they even got started. I took a deep breath and checked myself in the tall, oval mirror I kept in the corner of my room. I took in my appearance briefly, just to make sure nothing about me seemed off. Isaiah was one of those guys who picked up on negative energy, and I didn't want any coming from my body. The pink off-the-shoulder blouse I was wearing stopped just above my navel, and I turned slightly to check out my butt in the light-wash boyfriend jeans hugging my hips.

"Nice," I said, admiring my best feature. "All right, Matise, it's showtime!" I made it to the door just as Isaiah knocked again, and I swung it open.

"Dang, woman! I thought you had changed your mind."

"No, I'm sorry," I said and stepped out of his way. "Come in. I was just trying to finish up some last-minute packing. I'll just be a second longer. Let me go grab my stuff."

When he was inside, I shut the door behind him and headed back to my room to grab my things. I hoisted my yellow and white floral duffle bag over my shoulder with a small grunt. Amara and I had stuffed all my beauty needs inside of it, including my foldable hair dryer just in case I wanted to straighten my hair. I then grabbed the two matching suitcases by the extendable handles, flicked off the light, and left my bedroom.

"Can you help me with all of this stuff?" I asked.

"You said that like you're bringing your whole clos . . . Damn, Te Te!" Isaiah's eyes got big when he saw all my luggage. "We're going across town, not to Dubai!"

"I know," I giggled. "But a girl can never have enough things when going on an adventure."

"Oh, is that what we're calling this weekend?" he said, taking the duffle bag from my shoulder and pulling me close.

Did I mention how fine he was? Goodness. That man could steal rice from a China woman with just a smile. Not to mention how sexy he looked in his casual clothes. A simple Champion T-shirt and joggers did wonders for his physique. He raised my chin and planted a nice, warm, soft kiss on my ready and waiting lips.

"Mmm," I moaned into his mouth and smiled. "Yes, an adventure. Especially since I don't know what you have planned."

"Do you trust me?"

"If you're asking me, I'm questioning if I should." I raised my eyebrow at him. "Don't tell me you signed us up to do something crazy like skydiving, Isaiah, because if you did, I'm not go—"

"Relax!" He laughed and kissed me again. "Just come along for the ride, okay? Are you down or what?"

"Yes, under one condition."

"What's that?"

"That you take all of my luggage to the car."

"That's all? I was going to do that anyway," he said and winked at me. He grabbed the other two suitcases from the ground like it was nothing, even though I knew they were heavy. "Get the door for me, baby."

I did as he asked and gave my home a last once-over before I cut out the lights and followed him. I felt like it was the first day of the rest of my life, and technically it was. Nothing was the same. Everything had changed. On the way out and in the car for most of the ride, I thought about my relationship with Jordan. I didn't know where we stood or if I even wanted to stand anywhere with him.

"What's on your mind?"

"Huh?"

My eyes had been staring out the window, but when I heard his voice, I turned my head to face him. He glanced at me, taking his attention off the road briefly, and I saw the concerned expression on his face.

"You've barely said a word since we left your place. Everything good?"

"Yeah." I nodded my head and cleared my throat. "Yes, everything is fine. I just have a few things on my mind, that's all."

"Are you second-guessing spending the weekend with me?"

The sadness dripping from his voice was what made me reach out and grab his hand without thinking about it. I rubbed it with my thumb gently and shook my head. "No, baby, that's not it at all. I will admit at first I was skeptical, but now I'm really happy to be spending all of this time with you."

"Then what has you so quiet over there?" he said and looked at me again.

"I . . ." I sighed, not believing that I was really about to tell him. "My best friend is getting married."

"What?" he said with a smile. "That's what has you in a bad mood? I thought that was something to be happy about."

"It would be," I said, removing my hand from his and leaning back into my seat. "Except he hid the entire relationship from me. All six months of it."

"Yo! Six months? He's basically marrying a woman he just met! You're talking about Jordan, right?"

"Yes, him." I'd told him a little about Jordan in the past. By a little, I literally mean his name and the fact that we'd been friends since we were younger.

"Well, in his defense, maybe he really likes the girl. I've seen men fall head over heels over chicks before."

"Did they last?"

"Well, no."

"Exactly. Plus, Jordan has never been the type to fall head over heels. Girls fall head over heels for his potential and his money. Trust me, I've seen it all before. Then Lia came to my job this week."

"Who is Lia?"

"His fiancée, I guess."

"She . . . she came to your job? If you don't like her, why would you invite her here?"

"I didn't! Apparently, Jordan told her where I worked, and she just popped up on me."

"Well, what happened?"

"Nothing good. She wants me to help decorate the wedding, I guess."

"You gonna do it?"

"Hell no! Why would I decorate and design a wedding that I almost didn't know about?"

"Because he's your best friend. I don't agree with him keeping secrets from you, but I do see that he's trying to make it right."

"By what? Sending his girl to press me?"

"You want my advice?"

"No."

"Well, I'm going to give it to you anyway. Decorate the wedding."

"What?"

"He's your oldest friend, right? At the end of the day, if his marriage crashes and burns, it's on him. I understand that you're hurt, but two wrongs don't make a right."

I groaned loudly and pressed my head into the headrest of my seat. Why did he have to be so perfect? Even more, why did he have to be right? I closed my eyes for a second before inhaling a few fresh breaths and reopening them.

"Okay. Okay. I'll decorate the stupid wedding."

Chapter 5

Isaiah

"Are you keeping her busy?"

Placing his hand over the phone, Isaiah leaned back from where he stood in his kitchen and peered over the island. Matise was sitting with a small smile frozen on her face as she sat cross-legged on his leather sectional, staring at the television. The flat-screen TV was so big that it covered the entire wall, and the surround sound probably made her feel like she was a part of the movie she was watching.

It had been a long day. He was sure that she was still buzzed from the bottle of wine she drank at the restaurant they'd gone to for lunch after visiting the Museum of Modern Art. When he was positive that her attention was elsewhere, he put his cell phone back to his ear. "Why are you calling me?"

"To make sure everything is going according to our plans," the voice on the other end of the phone said.

"Everything is fine. I haven't lost sight of the mission yet. Have you?"

"Of course not! But I need her happy if this is going to work. It's been six months, and it seems that you haven't made much progress getting her to let her guard down."

"She's happy!" Isaiah said a little too forcefully, and there was a long pause.

"Hmm, could it be that you are really falling for her, Isaiah?"

"No," Isaiah said and glanced once more at Matise's beautiful profile. "She's just a job to me. And what do you care if she's happy?"

"Because when she's unhappy, Jordan is unhappy. But if you're saying she's happy, then good. Make sure you keep that energy. We are too close to the finish line for any mix-ups. I would hate for there to be any unnecessary casualties this time."

"I understand. Was there anything else that you needed?"

"I see you got her to agree to decorate the wedding."

"I did. You don't sound very happy about it."

"I'm starting to see that she is more of a problem than I thought, that's all. She's too important to him."

"It's looking like your plan to keep her in the dark is backfiring on you."

"Not at all. There are just a few bumps in the road I'm getting over. Speaking of bumps in the road, there is something that you may need to know."

"What is it?"

"Isaiah!" Matise called from the living room. "You're missing the good part in the movie, baby!"

"Here I come!" he called back and then turned his attention back to Lia. "It will have to wait. I'll give you a call later."

"Perfect. Be sure to call me. And, Isaiah? Keep her happy."

"You mean the way you did when you popped up at her job unannounced?"

"It was necessary."

"If you said you want to keep her happy, why are you doing things to upset her?"

"To push her closer to you. See, she had no one else to run to but your open arms. You should be thanking me. I know what I'm doing. Do me a favor?"

"What?" he asked, growing impatient.

"Be sure you're with her when she comes next weekend."

"Why?"

"Just be here."

Lia disconnected the call on him just as he opened his mouth to ask some more questions. He groaned and squeezed his phone in his hand before setting it down on the counter by the sink. Going into business with his cousin had been one of the most beneficial things he had done in his life, but it was also one of the most nerve-racking. She was a control freak because she was the brains of every operation, but she couldn't pull anything off without him.

Lia was his mother's niece. His family had taken Lia in after her parents died in a fire when she was sixteen. She was young, but she had the shape of a grown woman, and maybe that was why Isaiah's father couldn't keep his hands to himself. At first, Isaiah didn't believe Lia's claims, but when he saw his father leaving Lia's room late one night, he knew it was true. His first thoughts had been to tell his mother what he'd seen, but when he told her, she didn't seem surprised in the slightest.

"Better her than me," she'd said in a drunken slur and chuckled up at him. "Why do you think I took her in after LeeAnn died? He always had a soft spot for my sister. I only wanted him for his money anyway. And I got it. She just needs to be happy that I didn't let her go to one of those foster cares. You too. You think Danny would let you or me stay if he found out you weren't really his?"

Her laugh afterward would play in his head for years. He didn't know why he expected help from the woman who let his father beat the crap out of him whenever he got too drunk. He realized then that he had never really known his parents, and he had to take matters into his own hands. His entire life he had felt a disconnect from the man he had known as his father, but he could never put his finger on it. They weren't alike in any way, but Isaiah always thought that was because he was the spitting image of his mother, Karen.

Isaiah knew his father had a life insurance policy that named him and his mother as the beneficiaries if anything were to happen to him. He also knew that there was a will in place for all his father's assets. His mother didn't have anything, not even a bank account, but she would have to go too.

Isaiah and Lia devised a plan to make their deaths seem accidental. It was no secret that both had an addiction to alcohol, so Isaiah used that to his advantage. His father would get pissy drunk alongside his mother every Friday night when he was off work, and the two would pass out in the living room. Once they were passed out and unresponsive, Isaiah and Lia entered with gloved hands, cut rubber bands, needles, and laced heroin. Finding their veins was hard, being that neither Lia nor Isaiah had ever done it before, but eventually they did. Isaiah put a needle in his father's hand, and Lia put one in his mother's. The dosage they made his parents inject themselves with was lethal enough to put an elephant down.

The effects of the drugs happened not too long after. Their body's jerked before they began to foam at the mouth, and the cousins watched motionless until their bodies moved no more. It was done. Lia wouldn't be hurt anymore. After their deaths were ruled accidental overdoses, Isaiah was awarded his father's entire estate, including the house, which he sold. One would have thought the deaths of his parents would wear heavy on his heart, but they didn't. He felt free.

At age eighteen, $2 million richer, Isaiah decided to go to college and make something of himself. He majored in business and climbed his way up the food chain. Lia, on the other hand, was a completely different story. She was never truly able to rid herself of the horrors that his parents put her through. She struggled to graduate high school, and afterward, college was nowhere in her sights. She used her body to get what she wanted, and that proved useful to Isaiah. Her targets were usually wealthy, older men who had one thing in common: they were the owners and CEOs of the companies that happened to be Isaiah's competition. He used her to distract or blackmail them to sell shares of their companies to him. If they refused, then he would have to handle the problem. Lia would get a big slice of the pie for helping him to keep up the luxurious life she had grown accustomed to living.

His latest target had been an older man by the name of Jacob Heart. His business, J-Net, had climbed and was sitting comfortably as the third most profitable black-owned software company in the country. NYC Partners was number one. Although he had told Matise that he was a vice president in the company, the truth was he was the owner. She had become a casualty in a fight that she shouldn't have been in in the first place. However, six months prior, when Isaiah found out that Jacob would be retiring before the year's end and that he had already begun to transition everything over to his son, plans changed and so did Lia's target.

She moved from New York to Nebraska and quickly got a job as a secretary at J-Net. The rest was history. There wasn't a man alive who could resist Lia's charm, and that included Jordan Heart. There was only one thing that Lia seemed worried about, and Isaiah had never seen Lia worried. He had a close friend, a woman, who was a little too close. She asked Isaiah to keep her busy while she worked her magic on Jordan. The only thing was, and she would never admit it him, she had fallen in love with Jordan. She moved and made it seem like it was only business, but he knew better. She was too concerned with keeping Matise happy, and he knew that could only be to keep Jordan happy. Still, he figured he'd better get a grip on the situation before he fell down the same rabbit hole.

He finished up in the kitchen, turning the sink faucet on and off for effect, before going back into the living room. As soon as she saw him, Matise smiled from ear to ear.

"I missed you," she said and kissed him when he sat down beside her.

"I was only gone for a few minutes," he said, returning her smile.

"A few minutes too long. Everything good?"

"What do you mean?"

"I heard you on the phone. It sounded like you weren't happy for a second."

"You have good ears," he said. "But yes, everything is fine. My cousin just called me asking for money. Every time I help her out, she goes through the funds like water."

"Sounds to me like you might need to cut her off. Sometimes a helping hand turns into an enabling one."

"I couldn't agree with you more, but she had a hard life. My parents took her in when she was young, and I've been looking out for her since. Some may call it enabling. I call it spoiling. Kind of like what I want to do to you."

His eyes lowered as she stared at him with fond eyes.

"I like you more and more every day. It's not too often that a girl comes across a guy like you."

"Well then consider yourself lucky," he said and nestled his head in her neck. He inhaled and smelled the sweet scent of Burberry eau de parfum that he'd gotten her. "Now, I hope there is still some wine in your system."

"And why is that?"

"Because you get so nasty when you're drunk." He put his hands in between her legs and applied pressure where he knew she'd like it. "Did you have fun today?"

"Yes," she said in a low tone as he pulled her low-cut blouse down even lower.

"You did?" he asked seductively and popped one of her breasts out and exposed her nipple.

The moment he saw her brown areola he felt himself get a hard on. She had the most perfect breasts. They were soft, plump, and perky, just the way he liked them. He was tired of speaking with his voice. His tongue had a few things to say. He licked her nipple like an ice cream cone and felt her body give a small shiver. He licked a few more times, pulling her blouse down some more to free her other breast so that he could squeeze it in his free hand. When he wrapped his lips completely around her areola and sucked, Matise let her head fall back into the couch, and she moaned softly. Her hands encouraged him to keep going as they massaged the back of his neck and pulled him closer into her. He continued to lick and slurp, switching from nipple to nipple until she became relentlessly squeamish under him.

"Hsss," she hissed when she felt him bite down, and her nails dug into his neck. "You're making me so wet, Isaiah."

He didn't answer. Instead, he buried his head between her breasts and forced her to lie back. When she was lying down on the sectional and he was gazing down at her, he admired her beauty. Somehow, they always ended up making love on the couch, and that was because when he wanted her, he had to have her right then and there. He removed her blouse and bra completely and planted kisses on her from her chest all the way down to her navel. While he was kissing her, his hands had already unbuttoned her pants and pulled them down.

"How do you want it?" he asked as he tossed her jeans to the side. "Do you want it hard or slow?"

"I don't know. I just want you to fuck me, Isaiah," she breathed and opened her legs wide. "I want you to take it, baby."

He looked down at her pink cotton panties and licked his lips when he saw the wet spot right where her opening was. Moving them to the side, he slid a finger up and down her pussy, listening to the wet sounds of her juices. It was as if all the blood had rushed to his crotch, and as much as he wanted to taste her, he was so horny and needed her lips wrapped around his shaft. In one swift motion, his sweats were pulled down just enough to release his bulging erection and muscular butt. Positioning the tip at the opening of her womanhood, he leaned into her and kissed her deeply. She kissed him back sloppily, and her thirst for him made his first thrust the best he'd ever felt.

Matise was so wet, and her walls fought against his thickness, but he won the battle. Her screams soon drowned out the surround sound in the living room as Isaiah plummeted into her without mercy.

"You said you wanted me to fuck you, right?" he panted and leaned up so that he could watch her titties bounce.

He placed his hands behind her thighs and forced her legs up higher and wider. He had the perfect view of his dick sliding in and out of her creamy love tunnel. His own moans paired with hers, and he wished that moment could last forever. He wasn't just penetrating her sex. He was penetrating her mind. He could tell because normally Matise would fuck him back. She never submitted to him completely because she was a woman who liked to have control. But right then she just lay there and let him have his way with her, and that alone lit an everlasting fire inside of him. He was giving her the most powerful thrusts that he could muster to see if she would run, but she just kept taking them with her face twisted in a grimace of pleasure. She had one hand up by her head, and the other was on her stomach.

"It's so deep, baby," she cried out. "What are you doing to me?"

"What you asked," he said and pulled out. "Now come suck this dick."

His tone was aggressive, and he didn't think she was going to oblige, but she was on all fours in a matter of seconds. She opened her mouth wide, and he grabbed a fistful of her hair before he crammed his entire manhood down her throat. She gagged, but that didn't stop him from fucking her face as fiercely as he had done her pussy. Matise didn't back down. Her tongue found a rhythm, and so did her pretty, full lips. Soon, she was sucking him off so good, he was frozen in place with his head thrown back in pure bliss. It was like he was seeing stars, and when she put his balls in her mouth it felt as if he were about to explode, but he refused to do that without her. He leaned back and motioned for her to put her fat cat on his face so that he could pleasure her while she was doing it to him.

"I felt that jump," she said mischievously as she lowered her bottom toward his face. "I bet I make you cum before you make me."

"You must have forgotten what kind of skills this tongue possesses."

"No, I d . . . Oh, Isaiah!"

Her smack talking quickly turned back into screams when he gripped her by the waist and forced her down on his face. He rubbed his entire face in her wetness before taking her clit completely in his mouth. He sucked it like a Jolly Rancher, only it tasted much sweeter. Her mouth found its way back around what it was supposed to be around, and they gave each other head until they both had powerful orgasms. Her juices trickled down her thighs as she shook violently on top of him, but he licked them all up. His legs tensed up as he shot his nut out, and he felt her throat muscles going to work as she swallowed every drop.

"Shhit!" he shouted and kissed her inner thighs. "Damn, girl."

Matise crawled down and turned around so that she could lay her head on his chest. She said nothing, but she didn't have to. The two of them caught their breath together, and Isaiah wrapped his strong arms around her. He felt a surge of emotion go through him, and it caught him off guard. Was Lia right? Was he catching real feelings for Matise? No, he couldn't be. Like he'd said, she was just a job. A job that made him feel things no one ever had in his entire life. The more time he spent with her, the more he wondered whether, after he and Lia got what they ultimately wanted, he would be able to let her go. The answer to that question was one he didn't know, and that was what frightened him.

Chapter 6

Jordan

After he hung up the phone with Matise, Jordan's blood was boiling. Not only had she hung up in his face but she didn't answer when he tried to call her back. And did she say that she had a boyfriend? When had that happened? How could she be upset with him about not telling him about Lia when she hadn't told him about the joke she was seeing? He was fuming, and when Lia entered the bedroom they would soon share, she could see it all over his face.

"Is everything okay, honey?"

"I'm fine," he snapped, and when he saw her taken aback expression, he softened his tone. "Everything is good."

"Are you sure? Because it sounded a lot like you were arguing with Matise."

"Are you eavesdropping on my conversations now?" he asked, feeling his irritation flutter even more.

"Kind of hard to eavesdrop when you're talking so loudly that I can hear you in any part of this house."

Jordan groaned. He was being a jerk, and he knew it. Lia hadn't done anything to him. He approached her with his arms out and pulled her close. She was looking beyond lovely as usual in a white spaghetti-strap sun-dress, an oversized hat, and open-toe heels with ankle straps. He enjoyed seeing her wear white because it gave him a sneak peak of what she would look like walking down the aisle toward him.

"I'm sorry, babe. I just don't understand why she's being so hardheaded. This mess is getting ridiculous."

"I'm sorry, my love," Lia said and pouted up into his face. "And I probably made everything worse by popping up on her the way that I did."

"No, don't apologize. Your intentions were good, and your heart was in the right place. That girl is just stubborn. She said . . ." He stopped and let a heavy breath out. "She said that she isn't coming to the wedding."

"Well, would that be so bad? Do you want that kind of negativity at your wedding?"

"Yes, it would be bad," Jordan said and let Lia go. "She's my best and oldest friend, Lia. All this shit just isn't sitting right with me. Maybe we need to push the wedding back."

"What?" Lia asked, alarmed, and she cleared her throat. "You mean to tell me that you would push back our wedding to appease her?"

"Not to appease her. To figure some things out."

"Things like what? Didn't you say that as your wedding gift your father was signing the company over to you? Why would you want to sabotage your future because one person can't respect that you're in love?"

"She's just never been this mad at me, okay? Not for this long."

"Has it ever crossed your mind that maybe she's acting like this because she's in love with you?"

"What?" Jordan looked at Lia like she was out of her mind. "Matise doesn't look at me like that, Lia." He moved past her and made his way toward his closet. His father had asked to meet with him at work for a few hours, even though he was normally off on Fridays. Knowing that basketball shorts and a T-shirt would not cut it as work attire, he figured he'd better change clothes before he left. Jordan was a man all about looking good. It was something that Matise always teased him about, but it was something that he couldn't help. "It's not a crime that I like to look fly," he would always say in his own defense.

His fly-guy habits were what led him to purchase the house with the biggest walk-in closet that he could find. He was a firm believer in first impressions, and he always wanted to match that first with the second and third. When Jordan left his house, he was dapper whether he was in jeans and a button-up or a work suit. However, with a body like his, most women didn't care what he wore. Most of them would honestly prefer to see him naked.

That day was different from most. He was in a rush. The phone call with Matise had taken up more time and energy than he had anticipated. He flicked on the light in his closet and grabbed the first tan khakis and short-sleeved light yellow Gucci button-up he saw. He matched the clothes with a pair of chestnut brown and tan Gucci loafers and a pair of checkered Gucci socks. Jordan could feel Lia's eyes watching him like a hawk until he stepped out of the closet.

"Gucci down, huh?" she asked. "And where are you going?"

"My pops asked me to stop by the job for a few hours."

"I thought you were off today. I was really looking forward to spending the day with you since I didn't get to see you yesterday. And don't we have dinner with your mother planned this evening?"

"I was, but he called me and told me that he had someone big stopping by the office. Since I'm going to be taking over soon, it's important for me to be there. I won't be gone that long, baby." He kissed her tenderly on his way to the master bathroom. "And as far as dinner with my mom, that is still on. You go pick her up, and I will meet you guys at the restaurant. The reservation is for five-thirty, okay?"

"Okay," he heard her say, but he was already in the bathroom shutting the door behind him.

He took a shower and got dressed as fast as he could. It was pushing one o'clock, and he had told his father he would be there by one-thirty. Being that he lived in the Bennington suburbs of Nebraska, it would take him a little over twenty minutes to get to work downtown. The look that Lia gave him when he walked out the front door told him that she wasn't at all pleased with him and he most likely hadn't heard the last of it. But that would have to wait until later, since he was positive that she would be staying at his house that night. Although she had her own apartment in West Omaha, she spent most of her nights with him. She said that she wanted to practice living with him to make sure that it was something they both could do, and so far everything had gone smoothly.

She had started to redecorate the home to fit her own personal likes, and truth be told, he didn't mind it one bit. He loved her, and seeing her happy made him happy. He had to admit, he was the last one anyone would expect to settle down. He'd even shocked himself, but he'd seen a lot and done a lot. Lia brought a sense of stability to his life, and that stability brought him peace. She was the only woman in his life besides Matise who could make him laugh until tears were brought to his eyes.

It was a shocker to him that she and Matise hadn't hit it off. He had never forgotten about the day he had asked Matise who she thought his dream girl was. Lia was all the things that she had described that night, so he just didn't understand. He sighed and shook his head. He loved Lia, but the bond that he and Matise had was unmatched. He would stall the wedding out not only until she agreed to help with the plans, but until she agreed to be his best man. Well, woman.

As he drove his all-white 2018 Audi R8, his body seemed to function on its own getting him to where he needed to be. He was so lost in his own mind that when he parked in his designated spot at J-Net, he almost questioned how he had even gotten there. He grabbed his leather briefcase from the passenger seat before he got out of the car.

It was a beautiful summer day in Omaha, and that meant that the downtown was booming with people. It was one of the best features the city had to offer, and he was happy that his father had placed his business in such a beautiful part of town. Jordan walked through the glass rotating doors of J-Net with five minutes to spare and ran right into his father, and he was not alone. Standing next to him was a well-dressed black gentleman. The way they were so engrossed in conversation told Jordan that he must have been the man his father wanted him to meet.

Jacob Heart was a man who didn't seem to age a day. His hair was still jet-black, and he frequented the gym to keep his body in shape. Without a wrinkle in sight at age forty-nine, he didn't look a day over thirty-five. Once Jordan was spotted, his father patted the gentleman on the shoulder and motioned toward his son.

"Just the man I wanted to see! Paul Teelson, this here is the man who is going to be taking the head seat at the table come July!"

"So, this is the infamous Jordan Heart!" Paul's deep voice boomed.

Paul Teelson had a head full of gray hair, but he had a youthful face, and that made it hard for Jordan to put a finger on how old the man was. He was dressed like he either had just stepped off a golf course or would be on his way to one when he was finished there. He held his hand out, and Jordan shook it with a nice firm grip.

"In the flesh," Jordan said, flashing a smile.

"Paul here is the CEO at Bancroft, Inc."

Suddenly Jordan knew why his father felt that it was imperative for him to be there. Bancroft was the company that J-Net had been trying to close with for the past year, and it seemed that they were ready to make a merger deal. When that happened, that would give J-Net expansion opportunities into almost every state in America. There would be some downfalls, like the fact that their stock would go down briefly from acquiring a new company, not to mention the morale of all his employees. However, he was sure there would be enough incentives to keep everyone happy while all the kinks were being ironed out. The only thing left to do was to write their names in ink.

"So, Bancroft is finally ready to sit down and sign their lives away, huh?" Jordan joked.

"Seems that way," Paul chuckled and motioned his hand around the huge building. "Your father has done a superb job building this corporation from the ground up, and I think it's safe to say that I would be honored to be a part of it."

"Sounds good!" Jordan grinned at his father, who smiled proudly at him.

"Yes, yes, it does. There are a few things that will need to be hashed out, of course. But I plan to have an official answer for you by Monday."

"Take all the time you need," Jacob said. "I appreciate you meeting with me today."

"It's I who should be saying that to you," Paul said, and the two men shook hands in farewell. "And, Jordan, sorry I can't stay longer, but I'm sure I'll be seeing a lot of you in the future. Now, if you'll excuse me, there are a few golf holes calling my name."

He left without further ado, leaving the father and son alone to congratulate themselves.

"We did it, son! I knew twenty years ago when I started this company that we would reach this point one day!" Jacob let out a hearty laugh and gave his son a bear hug. "The only thing that has been on my mind is leaving this company in your hands better than it was when I started it. I know you're going to do a stand-up job as the new chief."

"Thanks, Pop," Jordan said and squeezed his dad back before pulling away with a grin on his face. "Answer me one question though."

"Shoot."

"Why did you call me here on my day off if you had already done all of the legwork?"

"If I don't get the day off, why should you?" Jacob laughed again and nudged his son playfully. "But no, I do have some things I need you to look over. They're upstairs in your office. They shouldn't take too long to mull over. I know you have dinner planned with your mother. I'd come, but I need to be here crossing all of my t's and dotting all my i's making sure our friend Paul signs the damn contract!"

"Understood." Jordan nodded.

"Before you go, how is everything coming along with Lia and the wedding?"

"It's coming along, I guess," Jordan responded. "Lia is excited about the new location, and Mom is, well, Mom."

"Yeah." Jacob smiled, shaking his head. "You know your mother has been waiting for this day all her life. And she seems to have taken to Lia the same way she did to Matise. How is Matise doing with everything? Haven't heard a thing from that girl since she walked out on dinner."

"You know Matise, hardheaded and stubborn. She told me that she didn't want anything to do with the wedding."

"Well can you blame her? She's been your closest friend for years, and you didn't even tell her that you were getting married."

"Not you too," Jordan groaned.

"Listen to me, son." Jacob placed a hand on his son's shoulder. "If I can offer you any worldly advice, let it be this: if the women in your life are happy, then so are you. It doesn't matter if it's your mother, wife, or best friend. If they have a smile on their face, then you did the right thing."

"I thought I was doing the right thing. It was Lia's idea to keep it from her."

"And why would you go along with some crazy shit like that?"

"I may have slipped up and told her how judgmental Te Te was whenever I dated anyone. But come on, you know how Te Te is, Pop. Lia wanted to keep our relationship low-key until we decided if it was real. By the time I'd figured it out that she was the one for me, I was enjoying the peace of Te Te not knowing. Now she's all mad at me, and every time we talk it turns into an argument. I want her at my wedding, but at this point, I don't know if it's worth the hassle of trying to get her there."

"Well, son, I understand where you're coming from, but that doesn't change the fact that your best friend's feelings are hurt. Fighting fire with fire isn't going to do anything but burn the house down. And we don't want that. Plus, Te Te is like a daughter to me. Fix it, or you won't be getting that nice office facing all of downtown like you wanted."

"Pop!"

"Ah! Ah! Fix it." Jacob put his hand up as he walked away, letting Jordan know the discussion was over.

Jordan felt like a teenager all over again, and he smacked his lips loud. He didn't want to call Matise basically begging to be her friend, but then again, he really wanted that office. It was triple the size of the one he currently had. He battled with himself the entire journey to his office, and by the time he got off the elevator on the fifth floor, he'd made his decision.

He waited until he was sitting at his large wooden desk to pull out his phone. He scrolled through his contacts until he landed on the one with Matise's photo, and he hit the call button. He was positive that she was not going to answer, especially after their heated argument, and he prepared himself to leave a voicemail once it beeped. Surprisingly, after the fourth ring, she picked up.

"What do you want, stupid?" she asked tersely.

"You're so fucking rude, man!" he exclaimed, forgetting immediately that he had called to make amends.

"You have ten seconds, or I'm hanging up this phone."

"I have your spare key, remember? Hang up this phone, and I'll see you in the morning, hear?"

"Aw, so you're my dad now?"

"I didn't say that."

"Okay, sooo what is it that you want? Why do you keep blowing up my phone?"

"I wanted to call you and apologize," he said, and when she didn't respond for a few moments, he checked the phone to make sure they were still connected. "Hello?"

"I'm here. What are you apologizing for?"

"I guess for leaving you in the dark about my relationship. I had my reasons, but I understand why you're upset. But I want you to know that I love you, Te Te. No one could ever replace you in my life, and I know that I hurt you, but it would hurt me even more if you aren't a part of this whole thing. My entire life is changing, and I don't know what I would do if you weren't with me when those changes happen. I want you to be my best man, well, woman, if I can have you. What do you say?"

He held his breath, waiting for her to say something smart. On the other end of the phone, he heard her let out a long, breathy sigh. He could have bet his bottom dollar that she was rolling her eyes to the high heavens.

"Okay," she said. "I'll decorate the wedding and be your best whatever."

"Yes!" Jordan said and pumped his fist. He felt the happiness welling up inside of him. "So are we best friends again?"

"You sound like a fifteen-year-old girl," she laughed.

"Yeah, well you were acting like one."

"Was not!" she said defensively. "But yes, we are best friends. We never stopped being that. You just do some stupid shit sometimes."

"Wouldn't be me if I didn't. Do you think you can get time off from work to come home next week? I really want you and Lia to get a fresh start and start working together on this thing."

"Next week?"

"Please? It would mean a lot to me. Plus my mom was upset that she didn't really get to see you the last time you were home. It hurt her little feelings."

"Oh come on! Don't throw your mother into this! That's a low blow even for you."

"Pleaaasse?"

"Okay, I'll come. But only for Cynthia."

"And will you be nice?"

"I can try, but I'm not making any promises."

"I can take that," he said and cleared his throat. "So, about this boyfriend of yours—"

"Oh my God!"

"You said it! Not me," Jordan said, and to remind her, he mimicked her voice. "'Now if you'll excuse me, my boyfriend will be here any minute to pick me up for our romantic weekend getaway.' Spill it."

"I do not sound like that! And he's not my boyfriend. I just said that so you know how it feels when someone keeps secrets."

"But there is a he, right? Or is it a she?"

"Yes, he's a man, fool! He's just not my boyfriend."

"What's his name and profession, and how long have you been dating this man?"

"Damn, what is this, twenty questions?"

"I'm just doing to you what you have always done to me. So, answer the question."

"His name is Isaiah, and he is a vice president at a software company, so you guys actually have one thing in common. We've been seeing each other off and on for a few months, but we just recently decided to try the dating thing for real."

"Do you like him?"

"I do. He treats me well."

"Perfect, then you shouldn't have any issue bringing him with you when you come next week."

"I'll think about it," Matise said. "But we are out to eat right now, and I've been in this bathroom for a while. I'll try to call you later, okay?"

They said their good-byes and got off the phone. Not only had Jordan gotten his friend back, but he had secured his office, not that that was more important than Matise. But it was a great incentive. He picked up the pile of work his father had set on his desk and started to work on it with a smile on his face.

Chapter 7

Lia

It wasn't hard, faking like she liked Mrs. Heart. Not as hard as she thought it would be anyways. Normally she hated parents, but not Cynthia Heart. She was such a sweet and genuine lady who liked to see the good in everyone. Maybe that was why she hadn't sussed out Lia's true intentions. She had done nothing but welcome Lia with open arms and make her feel as welcome as she could.

"You look beautiful tonight, Mrs. Heart," she said with a sweet smile from where she sat on the opposite side of the table.

It was true. The older woman had aged as well as Angela Basset with the body to match. That evening she was in a peach capris pants suit with a low-cut white top under her short-sleeved jacket. Her hair was pulled back, showcasing her lovely skin and high cheekbones. Whenever Lia looked into her eyes, she saw Jordan staring back at her. It was like he was the spitting image of the woman across from her.

"Thank you. And as usual, you look absolutely stunning yourself. That white dress looks great on your skin."

Jordan had made reservations for all of them at Genji, a Japanese hibachi grill in West Omaha. It was five minutes past five-thirty, and the two women were waiting at a table by the bar for him to arrive so that they could be seated. He said that he was on his way, so hopefully, he wouldn't be too much longer.

"Thank you," Lia said and smoothed the dress down on her flat stomach. "I've been trying to stay away from white until the big day, but I saw this and just couldn't resist."

"I don't blame you. Oh! And speaking of white dresses, when do you think you'll be available to get fitted for my dress?"

Lia almost slipped up and asked her what dress she was talking about. She had completely forgotten that she'd suggested she wear Mrs. Heart's dress in her wedding. She was starting to regret that, but she could make up an excuse at a later time as to why she couldn't wear the dress.

"One of the weekends in the next few weeks should be good," she answered and tried to add a hint of excitement in her voice. "The days are dwindling. I need to get this show on the road!"

"Oh, yes! I think they're going faster than anyone would have thought. I already spoke with the caterer, so that's all set. I finally saw the ballroom that you two settled on."

"Really?" Lia asked. That time the excitement in her tone was genuine. "What did you think? I wanted something big and classy enough for both the wedding and the reception. That way our guests won't have to pick up and change locations."

"I loved it. I can only imagine how ravishing everything is going to look once it's all decorated. Oh, I do hope that son of mine makes up with Matise. She has an eye for that sort of thing."

Lia felt her face drop, and she didn't even try to hide her displeasure at the mention of Matise's name. She was sick and tired of that name coming up when it was supposed to be all about her. It was like Matise was a thorn in her side that she couldn't get rid of no matter how hard she tried.

"Did I say something wrong?" Mrs. Heart asked, and Lia sighed.

"Honestly? It just seems like everyone is more worried about Matise than Jordan having a good wedding."

"That's because Jordan won't have a good wedding if Matise isn't there," Mrs. Heart responded. "Those two have been like peas in a pod for as long as I can remember, and I can tell this little rift between them has been eating him up. Now I don't know what his reasons were for not telling Te Te about the two of you, but what I will say is that I've never seen her this mad at him."

"I tried to go visit her to make things right between the two of them."

Mrs. Heart raised her eyebrow. "I can only assume that didn't go over too well."

"She accused me of being after Jordan's money, and that hurt me, because I love your son. Plus I have my own money."

"Te Te is only doing what any good friend would. She has always felt a need to protect Jordan from anything that she felt was a threat to him. That is the main reason why my son should have brought the two of you together sooner. Now it's like she's being thrown into a sea of sharks."

Slowly, Lia could feel the warmth she had for Mrs. Heart begin to deteriorate. She was saying all the wrong things. Once again, someone else was babying Matise's temper tantrum.

"Well, personally I think she needs to grow up." Lia shrugged. "This is a time to be happy, and honestly she has been making things hard. Jordan hasn't wanted to discuss any of the wedding plans, and it's been putting us behind schedule. He's even talking about pushing the wedding back because Matise said she doesn't want to be a part of it. Is there any way that you could maybe talk to him? We can't push the wedding back so that he can talk her into coming. That's ridiculous, don't you think?"

"Truth be told, if he said he's going to push the wedding back until Matise agrees to come, then that wedding will be pushed back. That's his best friend, and there isn't enough talking in the world that could change his mind about that. If she's unhappy, then he's unhappy, and that is how it's always been. It used to drive me and her mother nuts, but eventually, they'll get it together."

"Well I hope 'eventually' is soon," Lia was saying just as Jordan walked through the doors of the restaurant. Her smile lit up the entire restaurant when she saw him. "So, you finally decided to join us."

"Sorry I'm late," he said when he reached them. He leaned down to give them both kisses on their cheeks.

Seeing that their complete party was there, the hostess finally took them to be seated around a grill in the dimly lit restaurant. There was a Caucasian family of four seated at the table they were led to. Lia noticed that the husband's eyes lingered on her a little bit too long, and she rolled her eyes inwardly. Men were so easy. All it took was the allure of sex to distract them, even if their woman was sitting right beside them. Jordan pulled his mother's seat out first and then Lia's so that they could sit down.

"Thank you, baby," Cynthia said when he took a seat across from the women. "Your father and I raised you right."

"No problem, Mama. Do you know what you want?"

"I think I'm going to do the steak and salmon," she answered after briefly looking over the menu. "What about you, Lia?"

"You know what? I think I'm going to do the same thing."

"Great minds think alike!" Cynthia turned her attention back to her son. "Your father said you came into work for a little bit today."

"I did," Jordan said, and his face lit up like a child's on Christmas.

"What's that look for? You look like you just found a dollar in your pocket that you didn't know was there."

"I'm not trying to jinx it, but I think we are finally about to close on the Bancroft deal."

"Oh, honey, that's great news!"

"Yeah, that husband of yours knows how to work wonders. Now, he's still mulling over a few things, but if all goes well, he'll be signing by Monday. And when that happens, J-Net will be the number-one black-owned software company in the States before the year is up!"

Cynthia clapped enthusiastically, and the look on her face showed that she was just as happy as Jordan. She reached across the table to grab Jordan's hands in hers, and she gave them a hearty squeeze. Lia could just see the pride illuminating from her smooth, golden brown skin, and she forced a big smile on her face as well.

"Oh my God, honey! That's . . . that's great!"

"Thank you. I'm happy about it, but this means that I definitely have to kick my own ass in gear, because I want them to see and feel that I am just as competent a man as my father."

"They will, you know why? Because you are! You may have your father's business savvy, but you have your mother's heart. And that right there makes you a double threat!"

"Mama, you're always gassing me up!"

"Because my boy can't run on E! Oh no, he can't! It's my job to make sure you're full in all aspects of life, so there is no doubt in my mind that you are going to take the company by storm!"

Lia tuned out their current conversation. The only thing that kept ringing over and over in her head was what Jordan had said a few moments ago. The number-one black-owned software company in the States? In that moment, her feelings for Jordan didn't matter. She suddenly remembered her mission and how displeased Isaiah would be with that news. Ultimately the goal was for J-Net to, for lack of a better phrase, get down or lie down. If they somehow surpassed NYC Partners, that would not be good for Isaiah's business, and that would not be good for her own continuous money flow. Oh no, there was no way that she would allow that merger to happen.

"I'm so glad to hear that, son, but now let's talk about that friend of yours. What's going on with that? You two never bicker like this, and it has been weighing heavy on my heart."

Her statement snapped Lia back to attention, and she waited for Jordan to repeat the same thing he'd said right before she came. To her surprise though, Jordan kept the same upbeat tone and pleased expression when he started to talk.

"We talked, and she agreed to help with the wedding."

"That's music to my ears!" she squealed, and Lia tried her best not to roll her eyes.

Their waitress finally made her way to their table and took their orders. Lia ordered a drink to go with hers, because she needed something for her nerves. Whenever Matise was brought up, it was like she got placed on the back burner, and it didn't matter that the girl wasn't even there physically.

"She'll be here next weekend to look at the venue and start helping you with the decorations, baby."

"Great," Lia said, and she didn't bother to hide the dry tone. "Hopefully she doesn't try to bite my head off again."

"She promised to play nice this time, and I think it's important for you two to get to know each other. Isn't that why you went to New York?"

No, Lia thought, but she didn't say it out loud. "I guess so."

"My dad made a good point. When the women in your life are happy, you're happy. And when y'all aren't happy, I'm stressed the hell out! I just want everything to be smooth sailing."

"Your father is a wise man! Happy girls, happy world!" Cynthia chimed in. "Isn't that right, Lia?"

"I would agree, but it seems like the only person's happiness that everyone cares about is Matise's."

Their chef finally made his way to their table before anyone could respond to her. She made sure to tell him that she wanted teriyaki sauce on her steak and salmon before she excused herself to the lady's room. Once inside, she made sure that no one else was in there to eavesdrop before she dialed Isaiah's number.

"Are you keeping her busy?"

Chapter 8

Lia

Lia waited the rest of the night for Isaiah to call her back. When he never did, she decided that it was time to take matters into her own hands. After dinner, she and Jordan went back to his place for a nightcap. A few shots of dark liquor and two rounds of sex put him into a sleep so deep that she was positive he wasn't going to wake up until late morning. She waited until she heard his soft snores before she threw the thick red comforter off her legs and climbed out of the California king. Draping her silk robe over her naked body, and grabbing her cell phone off the nightstand, she snuck out of the room. Her feet barely made any noise on the soft carpet. She made her way downstairs to the kitchen since he always set his leather briefcase on one of the stools around the island. She flicked on one of the lights in the kitchen so that it wasn't bright, but just lit up enough to where she could see what she was doing. Like she thought, the briefcase was sitting on the stool closest to the kitchen's entrance.

"Now where is it?" she whispered as she rummaged through everything inside of it. "Ahh, there it is."

Her fingers gripped a packet of papers and pulled them out so she could get a closer look. It was a copy of the contract between J-Net and Bancroft. There was a sticky note attached to the front page, and Lia read the words on it in her head. *Pending: Paul Teelson's signature. In town until Monday.*

Lia knew that if Jordan got that signature, then it would be bad for business, and she couldn't let that happen. She placed the papers back in the briefcase and contemplated trying to ring Isaiah one last time. She checked the time on the digital clock on the stove and saw that it was four in the morning. She didn't want to call him and risk causing friction between him and Matise, so she opted to dial another number.

"Hello?" a hushed voice answered on the other end.

"Did I catch you at an inconvenient time, Bill?" Lia asked in a candy-sweet tone.

"I just happened to be awake when you called me," Bill said, and Lia heard the sarcasm dripping from his voice. "What's going on?"

Bill, aka William Wells, was a CIA agent based out of New York. He was what most would call a dirty agent, but Lia thought otherwise. In a world of selfishness, one could only truly look out for oneself. Isaiah had pulled some strings on one of the cases Bill worked a few years ago, and that took down one of his competitors, so now Bill owed them a favor. Lia figured there was no better time to cash in on that favor.

"I need information on someone."

"Oh yeah? Who is this someone?"

"Paul Teelson."

"Paul Teelson?"

"Yes. I need everything that you can find on him, including his current location, before noon."

"Well this is pretty short notice, don't you think?"

"You better get on it then," Lia said and disconnected the call.

She exited the kitchen, flicking the light switch off behind her, and went back to bed. Jordan was still in the place where she left him, and when she climbed back in the bed, he didn't even budge. Her eyes fell on his sleeping body, and she watched him in the dark for a few moments. Dealing with him was the first time where she had to keep reminding herself that it was just a job. She had to keep telling herself that what they had was not real. She had been a woman who used what she had to get what she wanted, and she had been doing just that for years. It all started years ago when her parents died and she had to go live with her aunt. They were good people, or so she thought. At first, it was fine, but then she developed into a woman. It was one thing getting looks from men outside of her home, but it was another living with a predator.

Lia sat on her bed, waving her hands frantically in the air to dry the orange nail polish. It was eleven o'clock at night, and she should have been asleep since she had class in the morning. Her entire life had changed in the last six months since her parents died and she'd moved in with her aunt. There were a few adjustments that needed to be made, but it was finally starting to feel as if she fit in somewhere. She'd been given her own room, and her aunt had done an excellent job decorating it just for her. Lia felt that she was just trying to make her feel like she was at home. In school, she didn't really have any friends, but she preferred it that way. She was a loner, and when people got close to her, she pushed them away without even trying to.

When she was sure that her nails were fully dried, she reached for the soft pink porcelain lamp on her white nightstand and turned out the light. She didn't feel herself grow sleepy until almost twenty minutes of lying in the dark, but once her eyes shut she didn't open them, not even when she felt the dip in her bed. It wasn't until she felt the hand slide up her inner thigh that she awakened with a frightful jump. She whipped around to see who was behind her, and she scooted to the other end of the queen-sized bed.

"Shhhh," a voice sounded in the dark.

She didn't know why she listened, maybe because she was so shocked to see her uncle, Danny. He didn't have a shirt on, so his entire upper body was exposed. The moon gave the only light in the room, and with it, she could see the lustful look in his eyes. She pulled her covers up to her shoulders to try to hide herself, but he just pulled them back down.

"Why are you trying to hide yourself from me?" he asked.

"W . . . what are you doing in here?" Lia whispered in a scared tone. "I don't think Auntie would like this very much."

"What she doesn't know won't hurt her," he said and smiled. "You're so beautiful. Has anyone ever told you that? You look so much like your mother."

"Thank you."

"You're welcome. You've grown into such a gorgeous woman. Your body has developed. You have the nicest curves."

On the word "curves" he traced his middle finger on her hip. That time she didn't jump. She was too frozen in place. Her breathing became shallow as his finger traveled up toward her breast. When it flicked against her nipple, she was confused by the tingles that shot through her body.

"Have you ever let a man please you?"

"I'm only sixteen. I'm a virgin."

It was a lie, and she could tell that he saw right through it. He smiled and shook his head, letting his hand fell on the spaghetti strap on her nightshirt. Lia shivered slightly when he pulled it down. She couldn't believe what was happening. Even if it wasn't by blood, he was supposed to be family. He was a very handsome man who could have any woman he wanted, so why would he want her? She clenched her eyes shut when she felt his mouth around her nipple. It was wrong, and she knew it was, but she was too scared to do anything.

"This can be our little secret," he whispered as he forced her to lie down so he could climb on top of her. "Okay?"

Lia blinked the memory away. That was the first night of many that Danny snuck into her room and used her body to pleasure himself. That was also the day that Lia figured out the way to any man's pockets. After that, Lia never looked at men the same. It was never hard for her to throw them to the side after she used them for what she wanted. They were all disposable to her.

She never went back to sleep. As the sun came up and Jordan began to stir beside her, her eyes stayed planted on the ceiling above. She could assume that it was eight in the morning, and if that was the case, she had been wrong about how good she had put it on Jordan. No matter what, he was the early bird that got the worm every day, even on his day off. She felt his lips on her cheek as he bid her a good morning. Her lips said something back, maybe it was also good morning.

"Are you hungry?" he asked her as he got out of bed.

"I could eat."

"Breakfast in bed it is then for my queen."

"Your queen?" she said and sat up.

She had never heard him say that before. He turned back to her and cupped her chin in his hand. The look in his eyes was one that she couldn't describe, and she'd never had anyone look at her in such a way. Especially not as soon as they woke up in the morning.

"You're more than just that. You are the future Mrs. Heart, so that makes you everything. I love you, Lia."

She welcomed his lips to hers and allowed him to kiss her tenderly. She didn't mind his morning breath one bit, and a part of her wanted to pull him back in bed with her. She didn't. Instead, she let him throw on a pair of basketball shorts and go down to the kitchen.

The thing between them wasn't supposed to go as far as it had. How she ended up with a 5.25-carat diamond ring on her finger was beyond her. She was living a lie, and the deeper she got into it with him, the harder it was going to be when she hurt him. Because she knew it was going to come.

Ping!

Her phone gave a little vibrate from the nightstand and snatched her away from her thoughts. She picked it up with her pretty, manicured fingers and glanced at the screen. It said that a number that she didn't recognize had sent her a text, but when she opened it she knew exactly who it was. The smile that came to her face was slow and sinister.

"Thanks, Bill," she said out loud.

He had come through sooner than she had expected. Paul Teelson was staying downtown at the Marriott downtown, room 235, and was scheduled to check out Monday afternoon. She wanted to hop out of bed, throw her clothes on, and run to her apartment, but she heard Jordan downstairs bustling around in the kitchen, and she thought better of it. She could play the wifey role for a few more hours, especially since the next time she saw him he might not be too happy.

Click. Clack. Click. Clack.

The sound of her blue Alexander McQueen crystal-embellished satin sandal heels stabbed the ground of the hotel floor as Lia walked with a purpose. She knew exactly what she was doing when she switched her hips from the left to the right, and she had purposely not worn any panties so that she would have an extra jiggle. She smirked, seeing every eye fall on her, but she was only worried about a certain set of eyes. Finally, she reached the elevators, and she pressed the up button as if she had a room and was staying there. She waited patiently for the set of doors to open. She smelled him before she felt him stop behind her, but she didn't turn around. She knew he saw her. She could feel his gaze going up and down her curvy frame. When the elevator doors opened, she walked in, and Paul Teelson stepped in right after her.

"What floor, Mrs.—"

"It's Miss," Lia corrected him. "And I'm on the next floor up."

"Well isn't that a coincidence? I am too," he told her and pressed the button that had the number two.

"Oh really?"

"Really. Well, miss, what brings you here this evening? Are you from Nebraska?"

"Me? Oh no. I couldn't live here. It gets entirely too cold in the winter! I live in Texas. Just visiting family for the weekend. What about you?"

"I'm here on business. I do a lot of travel for work."

"What is it that you do?"

"I'm the CEO of a large company," he said and put his hand in his pocket. "We—"

Ding!

They reached their destination, but she allowed her eyes to remain on his for a moment. "You were saying?" she asked.

"I was just saying . . . that I would love to continue this conversation in my suite, if you're not too busy Miss . . . ?"

That was the second time he'd asked for her name, but instead of giving it to him, she smiled seductively up into his face. They were too easy, men were. There was the occasional one who didn't fall into the allure of sex, but not many. All Lia had to do was pump his head up to get him to do what she wanted. But no, that was too easy. Plus, she had always liked to play with her food.

"Just miss for now," she said, stepping out into the hallway.

"All right, miss, I'm Paul. Do you have any plans for the rest of your evening?"

"No, I don't."

"I have an unopened bottle Dom Perignon that I wouldn't mind sharing with a beautiful lady like yourself."

"Is that right?" She touched her tongue to the top of her lip. "You have a pretty tempting offer there. Lead the way."

He held his arm out, and she hooked on to it with her hands. His room wasn't too far off, and when they got there, he held the door open so that she could walk ahead of him.

"Nice," she said, looking around the apartment-like suite.

"It isn't Caesar's Palace, but it will do," Paul said, letting the door fall shut behind him. "Have a seat."

She did as she was told and sat patiently on the cream-colored couch in front of a flat-screen TV. She had the whole evening to toy with him. Jordan thought that she was looking at wedding gowns, and she didn't have to worry about him bothering her. When Paul brought her drink back, she took in his entire physique. His nice body made up for his graying head, and she wondered if his height meant that he had length in other places. He sat next to her, and the two of them clanked their glasses together before taking their first sips.

"But as I was saying . . ." Paul said and continued to speak about himself.

As Lia listened to him talk, she learned a few things about who he was. She could tell he was a man over-compensating for a fear of getting old. He didn't ask her much about herself, and she kept seeing his eyes flicker from the cleavage in her yellow blouse to her wine. It was obvious he only wanted one thing, and he was just waiting for her to finish her glass. When she got to the last drop, she licked it from the rim sexily.

"I'm interested in seeing what other tricks that tongue can do."

"Very forward of you, Paul."

"Well, I'm a man who's all about knowing what he wants. And right now, what I want is my face to be buried in your pussy."

"Kinky. I like that."

"You and I both knew what was going to happen the moment you agreed to come back here," he said and leaned in toward her. "The question is, do you want it in here or the bedroom?"

She gave a little laugh, and she had to admit, his asser-tiveness intrigued her a little. She grabbed his wine glass and downed the rest of it, before standing up and leading the way to the bedroom. She had a yellow clutch that, along with her cell phone, she set down on the bedroom dresser, and she turned to face him. He was loosening his midnight blue tie, watching her the way a cobra did a snake charmer. Her body moved seductively, enticing his trance, as she removed her clothing slowly.

"Do you believe in chance, Paul?" she purred and slid her skirt to her ankles. She then pulled her shirt over her head, revealing that she hadn't been wearing a bra, either. "Or what about destiny? I do. I believe that everything happens for a reason."

"Are you saying that I met you tonight for a reason?" he asked, dropping his own pants.

"Maybe," she said. She was pleased to see that the older gentleman was working with nice equipment. He was bulging out of his boxers, and Lia reached and massaged it. Paul let out a sigh and finished unbuttoning his shirt. He tossed it to the side, and Lia licked his exposed nipple while rubbing his manhood.

"And what might that reason be?" he asked breathily.

"You'll know soon enough," she said and let him go so she could climb on the king-sized bed.

Her heels were still on, and she twerked her bottom in the air. His hand slapped one of her exposed butt cheeks and then rubbed it tenderly. He did it again to the other cheek before he forced her to arch her back as deeply as she could. She heard plastic ripping, and when she looked back, she saw him placing an extra-large Magnum condom on his thick chocolate meat. Getting on his knees behind her, Paul did exactly what he wanted to do and put his face in her pussy. Opening her cat up with his left thumb and pointer finger, he used his other thumb to rub her engorged clit while he drank her sweet juice. She quivered slightly when she felt him replace his thumb with his lips. He was eating her pussy so good from behind, and she reached back, encouraging him to put a finger in her butt.

"So, you're a nasty girl," he said and did what she wanted him to. He worked two fingers in and out of her rhythmically. "Tight little butthole. You want my dick to go there too? Huh?"

Without warning, he removed his fingers and spit a big glob at the opening of her ass. She felt the elasticity from the condom at her hole, and he spit on his shaft a few more times before working his way in. There was a moment of pain before the pleasure took over. Jordan wasn't really into anal sex, but Lia loved it, and she could tell Paul did too. He gave her long and powerful strokes, and she took them like a pro.

"Oh, mister! It feels so good," she cried and added a few extra moans for effect. "Give it to me!"

He was panting so hard that he couldn't talk back to her. He was out of breath already, and it had barely been five minutes. She reached under her stomach and rubbed her own orgasm out.

"Mmmm!" she moaned into the sheets when she felt her juices come down.

Climaxing always took Lia to a different place. When she learned to appreciate it, it was one of the most beautiful feelings ever. Paul's hands clutched her hips, and he began to jerk behind her.

"Ughh! Shit!" he groaned with his head thrown back. "That was a big one."

He pulled his limp muscle from inside of her, and a poot of air followed it. Paul briefly left to go to the bathroom, and Lia heard the toilet flush. When he came back, he kept his clothes off but handed Lia hers. Walking over to his nightstand, he plucked two one-hundred-dollar bills from an envelope and tried to give them to Lia too.

"For your time," he said in a dismissive manner.

She pushed his hand away from her and stood up to get dressed. She almost laughed because he thought that she was a prostitute. If only he knew that she was worse. Way worse.

"I don't want your money, Paul," she said, smoothing her blouse down and fixing her hair.

"I do insist you take it, but if you don't want it, I'll walk you to the door."

"You want me out so soon?" She pretended to be shocked.

"I have work to do, and I'm sure you want to get back to wherever it is you need to be, miss."

"Just like a man," she said in an even tone and studied his face with her eyes. "Once you're done with us, you just move us to the side. Tell me, Paul, would your wife appreciate the fact that you just had sex with a complete stranger?"

"Excuse me?"

"You heard me. Your wife. W-i-f-e. You think I didn't notice you conveniently slide your hand into your pants pocket earlier to remove your wedding ring? How would she feel about that, huh?"

"Okay, you need to leave. Now."

"I'm sorry," Lia giggled. "It's kind of hard to take you serious naked. Mm, mm, mm. All of that nice equipment and you can barely make it ten minutes."

"I'm not going to ask you again to le—"

"Leave? Or what? You're going to call security on me? You see, that's not one of your choices, Mr. Teelson."

"I . . . I never told you my last name. Who are you?"

"My name isn't important," Lia said and grabbed her phone from where it was propped up on the dresser. It had been leaned against her bulky clutch the entire time, recording the whole scene. She flashed the phone at him before she stopped the recording. "But this is."

"What are you going to do with that? Blackmail me?" he scoffed.

"For a man who sleeps with random women in hotels, you're kind of sharp. That's exactly what I'm going to do. If you don't do everything I tell you to do, I'm going to send this video to that nice office your wife works at so she can take you for everything you have."

"I'll kill you, whore!"

He made to lunge at Lia, but she calmly pulled out a small handgun from her clutch and aimed it at his head.

"Or we can do it this way. Either way works for me. But I want you to know, I came here for one thing and one thing only. If I don't get what I want, I will kill you and ruin the lives of everyone you love, do you understand me?"

He looked from Lia to the gun and then back to Lia. "Okay. Okay. I'll do whatever it is you want, just please delete that video. I can't risk my family seeing me like that."

"That's what I like to hear. To my understanding, you are here to sign a merger contract with J-Net, correct?"

"How do you know—"

"Correct?" Lia repeated herself a little louder.

"Yes. But what does that have to do with anything?"

"Everything. You will not sign that contract with J-Net. Instead, you will allow NYC Partners to acquire your whole corporation." Lia pulled a neatly folded packet from her clutch and tossed it at him. "From here on out, we will own you. Sign. Now."

"NYC Partners? But they're our competition! I . . . I don't even know what's in this contract!"

"Those lower on the food chain are often swallowed by their predators. We will make sure that you are promoted for your part in making this deal happen and that you have any further accommodations you may need. I assure you there are many beneficial attributes to merging with NYC Partners, one of them being"—she cocked the gun—"you get to keep your head. Now sign."

Paul looked like a dog with its tail between its legs. His jaw was clenching tightly, and Lia relished the look of distress on his face. She liked being the one in control. There was once a time when men thought they were the ones with the power, but no, that wasn't true at all. The one thing that she had been used for had become her most powerful weapon.

Paul had no other choice. He had to sign. He found a pen in the drawer beside the bed and scribbled his signature in every place requiring it.

"There," he said. "I don't know what I'm going to tell the people at the office about this."

"You'll think of something, I'm sure. We'll be in contact," Lia said and waved the gun. "Now get the hell out of my way. But actually, before you do that, give me that envelope." She nodded to the envelope of money he'd taken the two bills from. He grabbed it and placed it in her hands. Glancing inside, she guessed that there was at least $5,000, and she smiled.

"Thank you, Paul. You just bought my wedding dress," she said and sashayed to the bedroom door. Just as she was about to exit completely, she looked over her shoulder. "And please let this little meeting stay between us. We wouldn't want anything to happen to those girls of yours, now would we?"

Her smile was sweet as a peach when she left him standing there looking dumbfounded. When she was out of his suite completely, she let out a big sigh. Isaiah would be pleased when he found out what she had done.

Earlier that day, while Jordan was in the shower, she hacked into his work laptop and made a copy of the contract between the two companies and changed J-Net to say NYC Partners. She also made a few other changes, altering the deal to fit the new needs. Now NYC Partners would stay number one, and Lia would still get what she wanted. The only thing was, she didn't know what it was she wanted anymore. Her job had been to get close to Jordan, but the closer she got to him, the more she hated the thought of having to let go eventually.

The night was still young, and Lia made the choice to go to her own apartment before going back to Jordan's. There were a few things that she needed to map out, especially if Isaiah was coming with Matise. There was no way that Matise could find out Isaiah was her cousin. She already was able to sniff out the scammer in her on their first real sit-down. Lia vowed to be not so easily read the next time. Lia had never been in the position to deal with another woman. She usually took care of them before they became a problem. In this instance, Matise was safe, and not just because of how close she was to Jordan.

It took her thirty minutes to get to her third-floor apartment. She had a nice setup given the fact that she barely stayed there. She didn't have a permanent address, being that she was constantly moving around. She was what most would call a nomad. She hated being in the same area for too long. That's how she felt before she came to Omaha, anyways. Life was so simple there, so calm. The eight months she'd spent there were probably the most peaceful of her life. She was trying not to get used to it because she knew she couldn't have it forever, but what if there was a way she could? What if there was a way to have it all and leave who she was in the past?

She didn't cut on any lights in her home when she opened the front door. The familiar scent of fresh linen hit her nose as her air freshener did what it was supposed to. It was a little chilly inside, but she liked it like that. She maneuvered through the darkness until she reached her room at the end of the hallway. When she was inside, she opened the door to her walk-in closet and turned on the light. Most of her clothes had been transported to Jordan's home, so it was practically empty inside. The only thing there that she wanted was what her eyes instantly fell on. She'd removed the shelves on the back wall so that she could make a homemade chart, a chart that had an eight-by-ten headshot of Matise in the middle of it. Around the picture, and connected with colorful string, was all the information that Lia had dug up on Matise over the last nine months.

Before any job, Lia did her research. She liked to know who was close to her target and why. It helped her decide who she was going to be when it was time to get into character. When her target changed from Jordan's father to Jordan, she had to shift gears. She'd already found out a few things about Jordan, but the one that caught her attention was that he had a female best friend. Lia called in a few favors and found out all that she needed to know about Matise. It was really by chance that the woman lived in New York. In real life, she and Matise were opposites, but that would mean that she and Jordan were opposite too. She couldn't have that. She had to become someone he liked, some-one he was already used to. Someone like Matise.

Lia started following Matise every day for a month before she moved from New York to Nebraska. She learned her favorite places to eat and what she liked to do. Sometimes she would even disguise herself and sit close enough to her to hear what Matise's coined phrases were. She even went as far as to make fake social media accounts to follow Matise. Lia studied her mannerisms and her style and learned what made her tick. Some would call it stalking, but Lia called it research, and it was what made her so good at her job. She didn't stop until she was confident she could easily gain Jordan's trust, and she did. But Lia knew the only way to keep that trust until every evil deed was done would be to earn Matise's trust too. Lia stared at the picture of Matise, and the way the photo had been taken it was like she was looking back at her. Lia smirked mischievously at the picture.

"I can't wait to see you next week, bestie."

Chapter 9

Jordan

Jordan was all grins walking into the office Monday morning. After an amazing weekend, he was ready to finish the deal between J-Net and Bancroft. Paul was supposed to be meeting with him to return the papers at nine o'clock that morning, and Jordan had dressed for the occasion. His cream button-up was so light that it was almost white under a bronze suit jacket. The fresh line his hair had made it obvious that he had made a recent trip to the barber. He even purchased a bottle of the finest Scotch to celebrate with shots. At nine on the dot, the phone on his desk began to ring.

"Hello?"

"Mr. Heart," his secretary, Angel, said. "There is a Mr. Paul Teelson here to see you."

"Send him in."

A few seconds later, Paul Teelson showed up at his door. He was wearing a two-button khaki suit, with the jacket hanging over his arm. Jordan couldn't read the look on his face, but all he was paying attention to was the paperwork in his hands.

"Come on in," Jordan ushered him through the doors, but Paul shook his head.

"This won't take long. I just came to drop these off to you," he said and handed Jordan the papers.

"All right!" Jordan said and started to look through them. "I'll have someone call you and set up a . . . Wait. None of these are signed."

"I know. Bancroft was not able to agree to these terms with J-Net. Instead, we have decided to turn our business ventures elsewhere."

"What?" Jordan shook his head slightly to make sure he was hearing right. "Come again?"

"Bancroft will not be signing on with J-Net."

"Is there something in the agreement that you're not pleased with? I thought we worked it to both our liking—"

"Our decision is final. Now please excuse me, I have a flight to catch. Good luck to you."

And with that, Paul was gone as fast as he had come. Just like that, everything had crumbled at Jordan's feet. How was he going to tell his father that the company's biggest project wasn't going to happen? He was so mad that he started punching the air with his fists. How could he be trusted to run an entire corporation if he couldn't manage to get one signature? Jordan dropped down in his seat and buried his face in his hands. It seemed like once he got over one hurdle, he was right at the next. The only thing left to do was tell his father. He wanted to stall, but the look Paul had given when he'd said that it was final made Jordan believe him. Jordan had to be a man, because business had to continue.

"Son!" Jacob's voice boomed through the receiver of Jordan's work phone.

"Hey," Jordan said.

"How did the meeting go? You're calling me with good news I hope."

"Actually," Jacob sighed, shaking his head, "he didn't sign, Pop."

"Wait, let me check this damn phone. My connection must be bad, because I thought I just heard you say that he didn't sign."

"He didn't sign."

"What the hell do you mean he didn't sign? What did you do?"

"Me? I didn't do anything! He came in with his mind already made up. Barely gave me any time to speak."

"I don't understand. Everything with that deal was perfect. We even came to an agreement on stock shares! It just doesn't make any sense."

"I can't wrap my head around it either. He was so excited to sign with us Friday, but when he was here, it was like he couldn't wait to get as far away as possible."

"Well, I'm going to call him and see if there is anything that I can do to sway his decision. We needed that deal! We took a big blow last year when Teracom's software hit the market. Now, thank goodness they crashed and burned, but we still suffered a major loss we're trying to make up for."

"I'm sorry, Pop. I didn't know."

"I know you didn't, because I kept it from you. With the wedding coming and all, the last thing I wanted you to be worried about was the financial difficulties of the company. But now you have no choice but to know."

"What was the loss?"

"Almost twenty million. And this merger would have made us that and quadruple it before the year was over."

"You should have told me! I could have come up with a plan by now."

"I know, but I just really thought that this Bancroft deal was going to go through. I guess in my old age I'm losing my edge. I should have been able to see this coming a mile away. This is why I'm stepping down. It's time for some new blood to run through these walls."

"I'm going to have to push the wedding back."

"What? Son, no!"

"I don't have a choice. I won't tell her the reason why, but with what she wants, it's going to cost money that the company might not have in the next year if we aren't careful. I would rather use that money toward an investment deal."

"You know your mother and I got married at the courthouse. We were young and—"

"Broke like a joke." Jordan smiled for the first time since finding out that the Bancroft deal had gone south. "And then y'all had me, and you were even more broke. I know the story."

"Well then you know that was the fuel to my fire on getting a start on this company. It's our legacy, son. Something that you can pass down to your kids and that they can pass down to theirs. That alone is why we can't fail. That is why we won't fail. Everything happens for a reason, and I just hope that this is all for a damned good reason."

"I'm going to spend the rest of my day looking into new business ventures that might benefit the company. I'll keep you posted. Oh, and I might be calling you from the hospital tonight."

"Why is that?"

"Because I'm almost positive Lia is going to try to kill me when I tell her about postponing the wedding."

After he disconnected the phone, he groaned loudly. There was only one person who could make him feel better in a time like that, but she was probably busy with her own job. He hadn't talked to Matise since they'd made up, but that didn't mean that he hadn't tried to call. She had probably been hugged up with her new boo. It was strange. Jordan hadn't really thought about the fact that Matise was seeing somebody. He didn't even think she dated, and if she did none of them made it past the first week. But the way she talked about this guy, it was clear that she really liked him. Spending the weekend with him? Matise wasn't even the type to spend the night at a man's house. She had to be into him to be doing all of that, and now he was about to meet the family. *The brotha must be putting it down in the bedroo—*

Jordan felt a pang of something shoot through him, but it was something he'd never felt before. It came the moment he thought about Matise and her man being intimate. He didn't know why the thought of her having sex bothered him, but it did. It bothered him almost as much as it would have if she were Lia. He furrowed his brow, because he didn't understand why suddenly his feelings were going haywire. He couldn't wait to meet the guy to make sure he was the right man for Matise. Although they were grown, that never seemed to stop her from butting in his business. The weekend seemed so far away to him, but he knew it would come in no time. In the meantime, he needed to come up with a new business proposition before J-Net suffered another loss.

Chapter 10

Matise

Words couldn't describe how nervous I was stepping off of that plane hand in hand with Isaiah. Not only had I just made the decision to get serious with him, but he was already about to meet the people dearest to me. But it was a good nervous. I knew that he'd lost his parents at an early age and that he had been an only child, but that was all he'd told me. I always figured it was a touchy subject, so I didn't really press the matter. Hopefully being around my family would bring some sense of happiness and normalcy to his life.

We walked through Eppley Airfield, wearing our comfy travel clothes—jean shorts and white T-shirts—until we reached the passenger pickup area. I started to scan the scene for Jordan.

"What car is he in?" Isaiah asked, and I realized then that he had no idea what Jordan looked like.

"Knowing him, probably his Audi. He loves that car. Yup, and I was right, there he is!" The smile that came to my face was contagious, because the moment he spotted me, the corners of his mouth were at his ears.

He wasn't parked too far away, and I helped Isaiah drag our luggage toward the luxury vehicle. Once he spotted Isaiah, his eyes didn't leave him until we had reached the car. Instantly I felt the tension in the air. It was so thick that you could cut it with a knife. It was like a stare-down of two alpha males to see who would back off first. When it was clear that neither had any plan of doing just that, I figured it was time for me to butt in.

"Jordan, I want to introduce you to Isaiah. Isaiah, this is my best friend, Jordan."

It took a few seconds, but Isaiah finally held his hand out and offered Jordan a peaceful smile. I looked encouragingly at Jordan, and he eventually took Isaiah's hand and shook it with a grin.

"So, you're the Jordan I've been hearing so much about."

"Good things I hope."

"As of late." He gave a playful grimace. "I can't even lie to you like that. Why would you do some crazy shit like not tell her you're getting married?"

"Man, at the time I thought it was the right thing to do."

"Listen," Isaiah laughed, "I haven't known her for even half of the time you have, and even I would never pull something like that."

"That's why you're my honey," I said and kissed him on the cheek. "Is there room in the trunk for our luggage, Jordan?"

Jordan gave me a funny look. Well, I thought it was a funny look, because it was only on his face for a brief moment. He popped his trunk so that he could help Isaiah load our belongings, and then we were off. I sat in the back and let the fellas have the front seats, plus I was curious to see how it would go. I'd never brought any of the guys I dated around Jordan because, well, I never really dated. This would be a first for not only Jordan but for everyone.

"So, I hear you guys just decided to take a crack at the relationship thing."

"Yeah, Matise is finally taking a chance on me." Isaiah winked at me through the rearview mirror. "I was starting to think the day would never come. Six months is a long time to be in the booty-call zone."

"Oh my God!" I exclaimed in the back seat. "Please don't call it that."

"Well, what else would you call it?" Isaiah laughed. "Bruh, she used to hit it and be out the door before the clock hit twelve."

"That's cold, Te Te." Jordan flashed a smile back at me. "Funny, I still thought you were wearing a chastity belt all these years."

"Ha-ha," I mocked. "Sorry some of us are a little more discreet about their sex lives."

"I mean, what can I say? I was a playa back in the day." Jordan shrugged.

"Key words being 'back in the day.' All that matters now is that you're about to tie that knot," Isaiah said, and the two slapped hands.

"Thank you! Everyone knows that every man has to get that shit up out of their system before they settle down. For real though, that's the only way to tell when you're ready to hang up your coat. When that fast life is no longer appeasing you."

"Facts on facts, my brotha!"

"Oh no," I groaned as Jordan merged on the interstate. "Don't tell me you two are bonding over the dog ways of men."

"So, I'm curious, how did you know that she was the one? When you popped the question, I mean."

Isaiah asked the question I had been wondering myself. What was it about Lia that was different from the rest of them? I hadn't been able to put my finger on it.

"I don't know. I just knew. There's just something about that woman that I can't shake, and I want to spend the rest of my life with her."

"That's beautiful, man." Isaiah nodded his head approvingly. "It's rare these days to see a man step up to the plate. Most would rather shack up and pop out babies."

"Nah, man, now that would never have been me. Plus, I'm still up in the air about the kid thing. But if it happens, it happens."

The thought of him having babies with Lia made me feel a dip in my stomach. I turned my head so that I could stare out of the window, and I focused my attention on the familiar scenery passing by. Being home fed my soul. There was something about little old Omaha that put me in the best head space. Don't get me wrong, New York was amazing, but everyone knew there was no place like home.

"So, Te Te, my mom and Lia are waiting for you at the venue. What do you say Isaiah and I drop you off and take the bags to the house?"

"The house as in your house?"

"What other house would I be talking about?"

"We booked a hotel already, though."

"Well cancel it. I insist that my best friend and her guest stay in my home. I have more than enough space."

I looked to Isaiah to see if he would back me up, but of course, he didn't. He just shrugged his shoulders when our eyes connected. I wanted to tell him how much I did not want to stay under the same roof as them, but then I would have to explain why.

"I don't have a problem with it," Isaiah told me. "I think it would be a good idea for you to spend some time with the bride-to-be."

I groaned.

"You said you would play nice," Jordan said with a reproachful tone.

"I said that I would try," I corrected him.

"Te Te . . ."

"Okay." I rolled my eyes. "We can stay with you. How much longer until we get to the venue?"

"No time. We're here."

I glanced back out the window and saw that we were pulling into the parking lot of a large one-story building. I instantly recognized Cynthia Heart's ruby red Lexus parked next to a blue BMW. Jordan pulled up close to the walkway that led to the front door of the building, and I hesitated to get out of the back seat. Just as I was about to change my mind, I heard someone calling my name.

"Te Te! Girl, if you don't get out of that car and get over here . . ."

I looked up to see Cynthia standing on the long sidewalk with her hands on her hips. She must have been waiting for my arrival. I knew it would be in my best interest to get out of the car, so I did just that.

"Have fun," Isaiah joked.

I made a face before I shut the door and walked toward the building in my red and white Chuck Taylors. I had been looking forward to relaxing after my flight, but obviously, that wasn't in anyone's plans but mine. When I got close enough, I embraced the woman who had taken to me like a daughter. When she let me go, she gave me a look, and I couldn't do anything but shake my head.

"Go ahead and say it. I already know it's coming," I said.

"You know what I want to say, but I'm not going to say it. But what I will say is that I'm glad you're here. I have been going crazy trying to put all of this together."

"Well I'm here to help now," I said and put my hands up for effect.

"That you are. Now come on, Lia's inside waiting."

"Of course she is," I said and followed her.

"The wedding and reception are both going to be in the ballroom upstairs," Cynthia said when we walked through the crystal and glass doors. "Lia didn't like the idea of having a wedding at a church and then everyone having to travel to another destination."

"Smart girl," I said, admiring the building. Once I walked through the tall doors to where the ballroom was, I saw instantly why the venue was chosen. It was big enough to easily host 300 guests, and it had beautiful gray and white porcelain tile flooring. My eyes admired the empire chandeliers that hung from the ceiling and the white pillars that went from the floor and all the way up to the high ceilings. The interior designer in me started going crazy putting together the perfect ideas.

My mind immediately went to an almost all-white wedding. White tablecloths would be a must to match the cocaine white walls. I could see the golden drapes hanging from the windows and maybe even custom vases with bouquets of tall white flowers in them as centerpieces. The tables would have to be positioned in a way that would face the front where the couple would wed, accommodate for a dance floor in the middle, and also be in perfect sight of the stage on the other end.

"I know what that look means." Cynthia beamed at me. "I can see your mind going one hundred miles a minute. What do you think?"

"This is truly a beautiful location. There is so much we can do with it."

"I'm glad you think so. That means we are in sync," a voice said behind us.

I turned around and found myself staring directly into Lia's eyes. We stood there in an awkward silence, but if I were her, I wouldn't know what to say to me either. Especially with how I had come at her the last time. With her, it wasn't because I thought she'd be bad for Jordan. When it came to Lia, I had been jealous of her position in Jordan's life. That wasn't fair of me to do, and if the shoe were on the other foot, I would be apprehensive.

"Look, Lia. I want to apologize for the way I acted when you came to New York. I realize now I was a little harsh to you when you weren't doing anything but trying to make things right."

"A little harsh?" Lia looked taken aback.

"Okay, a lot harsh. I'm just very protective of the things close to me. And that includes Jordan. I hope you can forgive me."

Lia raised her eyebrow at me and turned her lips up like she was about to lay into me with some words of her own. Just when I was sure the first "bitch" was about to leave her mouth, her lips spread into a big smile, and she grabbed my hands in hers.

"All is forgiven! Girl, if I were you, I would be mad too. Honestly, this whole thing is my fault. When Jordan told me that he had a girl best friend, I was a little skeptical because I know how mean women can get when someone new comes into play. And then when he told me how judgmental you were with everyone he'd ever dated, I just didn't want your perception of me to rub off on him. I just wanted a fair chance, so I asked him to keep us a secret from you."

Her honesty made me lower my guard for the first time since I'd met her.

"I guess trying to protect him from the bad turned me into the bad, huh? If I weren't so ready to count you out, then we wouldn't be in this mess in the first place. But all of that is in the past now."

From the sidelines, Cynthia was watching us with an approving smile, but she didn't butt in and say anything to either of us. For the first time in two weeks, I felt at ease with everything going on in my life. Maybe I had never really been in love with Jordan. Maybe it was just a childish fantasy that I'd held on to for too long.

"So, tell me what you are thinking," Lia said when she and I walked away from Cynthia so that she could show me every part of the ballroom.

"Honestly?"

"Yes."

"I'm trying to figure out why and how the hell you don't have a wedding planner."

"We did have one. She was supposed to be the best in the city."

"Well, what happened?"

"Creative differences. I was all about beauty, and she was all about themes. She tried to plan some sort of *Coming to America* wedding for us."

"Oh no." I shook my head. "That was a great movie, but no."

"That's what I said! I want something more—"

"Elegant," I finished for her.

"Yes! I'm thinking something mostly—"

"White?"

"Yes! I want it so white in here that it's blinding."

"I think we can make that happen. But I was thinking gold—"

"Drapes." She finished my sentence for me that time.

"Yes! To accent the walls."

"I like how you think."

We spent the rest of the time discussing her wants for the wedding. It shocked me how much in sync we were about most of the things we talked about. The vibe between us was good for the moment, and I had to admit, she wasn't as bad as I wanted her to be.

Cynthia ended up leaving to go home and tend to her husband, but she told us both to just call her if we needed anything. A part of me wondered if the only reason she had come in the first place was to be a mediator if she needed to.

A few hours passed, and by the time we were done talking we had designed the entire ballroom in our minds.

"Okay, I'll go ahead and start getting all of what you want, and I'll send Jordan the bill. Being that this is his big day, I hope he is okay with not having a price limit," I said, smiling mischievously from where we sat at one of the circular tables.

"Uh-uh! You are not about to have him ready to divorce me before we even say 'I do' with bills for fifty thousand dollars!"

"Just tell him that you're worth every penny of it."

"I'm sure he knows that, but I just don't want him to think I'm taking advantage of him, you know?"

Her voice sounded so sincere that I wanted to kick myself. I had accused her of basically being a gold digger, and there she was being thoughtful about the price of her own special day. It was my turn to take her hands in mine.

"This is your day. I'm sure he's not going to mind, no matter what the total comes up to. Plus, he would yell at me, not you."

We shared a laugh, and I realized that I hadn't checked my phone once since I got there. I was stunned to see that she and I had been alone for almost three hours. The time read almost four o'clock, and my stomach was growling like a grizzly bear. The only thing I'd eaten that day was a burger at the airport and the tiny bag of honey-roasted peanuts they gave us on the plane.

"I think that's enough for one day. We have all weekend to iron out most of this stuff, plus it sounds like you have a grown man living in your stomach."

"Girl, I need to eat something like yesterday."

"Do you like PepperJax?"

My eyes lit up at the sound of my favorite restaurant when I was in town. PepperJax had the best Philly cheese steak sandwiches I had ever tasted in my life. Not to mention their famous rice bowls were to die for as well. "Do I like them? Girl, that's my favorite!"

"Really? Me too!"

"Then let's go, shoot. You're the one with the car. That was your blue BMW out front I'm guessing?"

"Yes, that's me." Lia playfully threw her hair over her shoulder. "I call her Blue Fizz."

"Ooookay," I laughed.

We left the venue together and spent the rest of the day getting to know each other better. By the end of the day, I was confident that I had made the right choice by coming home for the weekend. Lia was good people, and I understood why everyone kept telling me that I would really like her. We had so much in common it was almost like we were the same person. I made a mental note to tell Isaiah thank you for talking me into getting on the plane. Now I said, "tell," but y'all know good and well I meant "show." The moment I got some free time alone with that man, I was going to rock his socks off. I didn't care whose house we were in.

Chapter 11

Matise

"Let's get out! Let's go downtown like we used to!" I suggested.

We were all in Jordan's huge living room, sitting around talking about different happenings in our lives. We all were sipping glasses of wine, and it was obvious that we all had a little buzz. I was sitting on Isaiah's lap, and Lia was on Jordan's. It was like the laughter hadn't stopped since Lia and I entered the house. Once Jordan and I got on our "remember when's," it was a done deal. We completely took over the conversation, and my stomach hurt from laughing so hard.

"Remember when I didn't know how to dance?"

"Boy, you still don't know how to dance!"

"Babe, nooo! You can't dance?"

"Don't listen to her, baby. I gets down on the dance floor."

"Yeah, when his feet trip over each other!"

Lia and I shared a laugh, and I heard Isaiah snicker behind me.

"Aw! You too? You're a traitor, man. We brothas are supposed to stick together."

"My bad, bruh. That visual just got to me for a second. You're too tall to be falling all over the dance floor."

We all laughed again, and I sighed in bliss once it died down. "We used to have so much fun here, man. The good old days! I miss them."

"Enough to move back?"

"Not that much. New York has given me so many new opportunities. Opportunities that I can't throw away. Plus, I've met some people I don't think I'm ready to let go of," I said and cupped Isaiah's chin.

"You must be talking about Amara," he teased.

"Duh, I'm talking about Amara!" I said and squealed when he wrapped his arms around me. "I'm just kidding!"

"Better be," he said and then put his lips by my ear to say something only I could hear. "I wouldn't want to have to spank you tonight for misbehaving."

"Mmm. Now, baby, you know I like that kinky stuff. I might start acting up just because."

I kissed him, not caring that we were being watched. Being with him right then and there seemed unreal. I never in my wildest dreams would have thought that it would be happening, especially in the way it was happening. But I was glad that it was. I tasted the bitter taste of the wine on his tongue when I slipped mine in his mouth. We kissed until I heard Jordan clearing his throat, and I was reminded of where I was.

"My bad," I said without removing my eyes from Isaiah's. "Sometimes I just get a little beside myself."

"I'm not complaining," Isaiah said in a deep, sensual tone.

"Well all righty then," Jordan said and clapped his hands. "Enough of that."

"Honey, leave them be. They can kiss."

"You call that a kiss? They were basically performing oral sex on each other!"

It came out like a joke, but the way Jordan looked at Isaiah led me to believe that it wasn't. *Is he . . . ?* No, he couldn't have been jealous because that just wouldn't make any sense. I cleared my throat.

"Well were we really about to hit up the night scene or what?"

"Yes!" Lia exclaimed and jumped to her feet. "I have been itching to let loose. All this wedding planning has got me all bent out of shape. Did you bring going-out clothes?"

"Not really," I answered. "I have boring stuff, and at home, I am not trying to step out unless I'm looking my absolute best."

"Same. Come on, I think we're the same size. Take a look in my closet. Boys, go start getting dressed."

I followed her out of the living room and to her "closet," which was actually one of the spare rooms in the house. She had so many clothes that if I didn't find anything to wear, I just wasn't trying. Looking around, I saw we had a similar taste in clothes. I wanted to wear or try on almost everything I saw.

"Oh my God, I feel like a kid in Candyland! You have so much cute stuff!" I said, holding up a red dress.

"Ooh, good choice. I haven't even worn that yet but go right ahead."

"Are you sure?" I asked.

"I probably won't ever even get to it. I have so much stuff in here that still has the tags on them."

"Good, because this dress is banging, and I know Isaiah would love to see me in it."

I went over to the tall, rectangular mirror in the corner of the room and held the dress up to myself. It had thin straps and was completely open in the back. It looked like it would stop under my knees, but I knew once my curves stretched the fabric out a little it would stop above them.

"You really like him, huh?" Lia asked, coming up behind me.

"Who, Isaiah? I mean he's cool." I shrugged and gave a shy smile.

"Uh-huh. Looks like you're really into him. He seems like a good guy."

"He's a really great guy. I don't know, I think we're just trying to see where this thing is going between us. But I do like him. He makes me happy."

"That's so sweet." Lia put her hand on her chest. "Maybe we'll be planning your wedding next."

"Whoa! All I said was I liked the man!" I laughed. "I never said nothing about jumping the broom with him."

"Mm-hmm," she said and made to walk away, but stopped abruptly. "I know you've only been here for not even a day, but has Jordan been acting different to you?"

"What do you mean?"

"I mean . . . I don't know how to say this without sounding insecure."

"Say it," I encouraged her.

"Okay, I'm just going to ask. Did you and Jordan ever have anything in the past?"

"Anything like what?"

"Anything, anything?"

"Oh!" I said, finally catching her drift. "You mean *anything*. No! Jordan and I have been strictly friends since we've known each other."

"You've never even slept with him?"

"No!"

"Really? Wow."

"You say that like you're shocked," I said, still looking at her through the mirror.

"You never wanted to?"

"No!"

"You said that kind of fast. Are you sure?"

"Yes! I'm sure." I tried to laugh it off. "Girl, I am not one of those friends."

"Okay, I believe you. It's just rare, you know. You two are both good-looking people. Most would have taken advantage of the friendship, if you know what I mean."

"Nope, not us." *But I wanted to. At one point in time, I wanted to sit on your fiancé's face until he had my pussy juices on his sideburns. I used to want to let him hit it from the front, side, and back every day and all night.*

"Te Te?"

"Huh?" Her voice had interrupted my thoughts of everything I had wanted to do to Jordan. But that was the past. Lia didn't have anything to worry about with me. Jordan and I were strictly friends, and that was all we would ever be.

"I thought I lost you there, Buzz Lightyear. Your eyes got all mystical and shit."

"Forget you," I giggled. "I'm about to go and hop in the shower. If I'm lucky, I'll be able to catch Isaiah before he gets out."

I winked at her and left the room. The wine had given me a buzz that I wasn't only feeling in my head. My clit was throbbing, and my tunnel was begging for some friction. I entered the guest room on the second floor that Isaiah and I were staying in. Sure enough, I heard the shower going and Isaiah's soft croons as he sang to himself. The man was sexy and could sing a little bit.

"You know, if things don't work out in the software business, you can always take up a singing career," I said, stepping into the shower behind him.

He turned around and smiled down at my naked body. He didn't have to say any words. We both knew why I was there. Given the fact that we were all trying to get out of the house, we probably only had a good ten minutes. But it was ten minutes that I would take.

I dropped on my knees, feeling the water hit my face like rain. I could smell that he had just gotten done washing up, but that just meant I was going to get his clean dick dirty again. Good thing we were in the perfect place to handle that. I opened my mouth as wide as it could go and wrapped my lips around his shaft. Pleasing him pleased me, and the second I heard his low moans it boosted my ego.

"Suck this dick, Te Te," he encouraged me. "Suck daddy's dick really good, okay? Put it at the back of your throat."

I did as I was told and made choking sounds for him. I slurped and gagged on him until he pulled it out and made me stand up. Turning me around, he slapped one of my cheeks.

"Hsss," I hissed at the sting.

"Lean forward and toot this thing up."

I placed my palms on the back of the tub, leaned over slightly, and stood on my tiptoes. He bent his knees and jammed his rock-hard manhood deep inside of my yearning pussy. I didn't know if it was me or all the water from the shower, but it was slippery. So slippery that Isaiah couldn't help but to give me deep and quick pumps. The slapping from our bodies touching was loud, and anyone who came into the room would know instantly what was going on. The moment I felt Isaiah jerk inside of me I pulled away and fell back to my knees to catch all his nut. I licked and swallowed it all up, sucking on his ball sack to make sure it all had come up.

"I'm sorry, baby," Isaiah said when I stood up. "I've been holding on to that one all day. I had to let it loose."

"It's all right," I said and wrapped my arms around his torso. "You have all night to make it up to me."

"And I will," he said and grabbed the washcloth he'd dropped while sexing me. "Starting now, let me clean you up."

The way he washed my body was enough to make me quiver and shake. Being with him was so beautiful, and I was starting to rethink the whole going-out thing. I wished I hadn't even suggested it because all I wanted to do was spend the rest of my night alone with Isaiah.

But there would be more than enough time for that. Plus, going out and having some fun was something I needed to do.

We finished up in the bathroom and got dressed. By the time I'd put my hair in a halo braid and slid into my heels it was almost ten o'clock. The dress looked even better on me than I imagined, and Isaiah didn't look so bad either in his black Gucci V-neck silk shirt and Gucci skinny jeans. By the time we went down the stairs, Jordan and Lia were there waiting for us. Jordan was once again giving me a look that made me feel awkward, but the sly expression on Lia's face might have explained why.

"Y'all were loud," Lia said and smirked at us. "Let's go. The night is still young!"

Chapter 12

Isaiah

The club wasn't really Isaiah's scene, but he didn't mind kicking back every once in a while. The girls had ventured out on the dance floor, and he hung back with Jordan. They had decided to go to a place called Caprix. Apparently, it was a new club in downtown Omaha and real hot at the moment. Everyone there was having a good time, and the DJ was doing his thing. He enjoyed seeing Matise having fun and letting loose. She and Lia were dancing and blending in with the younger crowd.

"You wouldn't even be able to tell that they hated each other last week, looking at them now," he said, tipping his beer toward the girls.

"Real talk, you would think they were the best of friends," Jordan said, shaking his head.

"It's a good thing though. The last thing anyone needs is them trying to rip each other apart," Isaiah said, tossing his beer back and finishing it. "Yo, thanks for inviting me, man. I would have never thought there were black people in Nebraska if I never came."

"We get that a lot," Jordan chuckled. "I always say that if you want to get the feel that a bigger city has to offer in a smaller package, come to Omaha, Nebraska."

He downed the rest of his drink too and went back to people watching. He was leaning with his elbows on the bar counter, and Isaiah observed him for a moment to catch his vibe. He'd noticed something was off with Jordan when they all had left the house, and it was like his mind was in a different place. A few people who must have known Jordan from around tried to speak to him, but he barely even acknowledged them. Isaiah cleared his throat and leaned against the bar counter too.

"What's up with you, Jordan?"

"What?"

"All these beautiful women around and everybody is having a good time, but you look like you don't want to be here."

"Honestly? It's because I don't. But Te Te wanted to come, so here we are."

"Yeah, she has a way of getting what she wants," Isaiah said with a small, sly grin.

"I heard," Jordan said and looked Isaiah square in the eye. "Listen, Isaiah, you're a cool dude, and I see why she likes you. But Te Te is one of the closest people to me. Don't screw her over."

"And why would you think that I'd ever do a crazy thing like that?"

"I'm just saying. I've never met any of the people she's dated. She never brought them around. Shit, I almost thought she was a lesbian. The fact that you're here says something about the way she feels about you."

"So, what are you saying?"

"Just . . . just be good to her, all right? Or you'll have to deal with me."

The look in his eyes matched the serious tone of his voice. Isaiah knew that his words weren't a threat. They were a promise. Unfortunately for him, though, Isaiah wasn't scared of either.

"Duly noted," Isaiah responded with a slow smile and called the bartender back over to them. "Can I get two—"

"Hennessy," Jordan finished for him. "Straight."

"I thought you were classier than that, man," Isaiah joked, trying to lighten the mood.

"Yeah, well with the past few weeks I've been having, I probably need something strong."

"Well, Hennessy it is, and you can put it on my tab," Isaiah told the bartender and turned back to Jordan. "Trouble in paradise?"

Jordan sighed and shook his head. "Nah, Lia and I are good. Well for now anyways."

"What do you mean by 'for now'?"

"It looks like I'm going to have to push back the wedding after all. She's going to hate me."

"I had no idea that the wedding was supposed to get pushed back in the first place."

"Well it wasn't, but with the way Te Te reacted, I was going to hold off until she agreed to be in the wedding. When the fire got put out, I figured I was in the clear, but I was wrong. A deal at work didn't exactly come through the way it was supposed to. They backed out at the last minute."

"Don't even trip about it, man," Isaiah said, already knowing what Jordan was referring to. He kept a straight face. "You win some, you lose some. Certainly, that's not a reason to change the wedding date."

"It is if I don't figure out a solution, and quick. My father tried to renegotiate the deal, but they weren't going for it. It's going to be a big hit to the company, and he doesn't know if he's going to be able to step down now."

"Step down?" Isaiah feigned confusion.

The liquor was making Jordan real lippy, but Isaiah wasn't complaining one bit. He didn't want to go into business with J-Net. He wanted to own them completely. So, anything to give him leverage or an edge was helpful.

"The company was going to be mine," Jordan continued. "It was supposed to be my wedding gift. He was going to sign everything over to me a few days before our wedding. But now my father is rethinking the whole thing. He's afraid that I won't be able to handle things on my own."

"And what do you think?"

"I don't know." Jordan clenched and unclenched his jaw. "Just when I thought everything was ready for takeoff, it exploded in my face. Not to mention the small financial hole we're in that I'm just now finding out about. I'm just starting to think it's best to hold off on the wedding until everything is everything again."

"What kind of financial hole are we talking about?"

"Twenty million," Jordan responded, and Isaiah whistled.

"Damn! Was somebody stealing from the company?"

"No. Another company put out software that crashed and burned after a few months. But those few months did damage that we haven't recovered from. The merger was going to fix all of that, and now that that's not going to happen, I don't know how we're going to get out of the hole. I'm sure we'll think of something, but that will mean my father won't retire anytime soon. So that will also mean that I won't get the company for another year or more."

By then the bartender had returned with their drinks, and the men thanked her. Isaiah picked his up and sipped it, feeling the burning sensation trickle down his throat. What Jordan had just told him wasn't going to be good for anybody, especially him. Lia thought that she had been doing Isaiah a favor by pulling that Bancroft stunt when, in reality, she could have potentially sabotaged things for the both of them. Granted, it was a friendly takeover, and it was one that made sense. However, things were different now. The next phase in his plan could not be orchestrated without Jordan sitting on the company's throne. It was his turn to clench his jaw as he was deep in thought. It took him all of one minute to figure out a solution to the problem. It wasn't something he wanted to do, but he saw that it was what he had to for the moment. He took a few big gulps of his Hennessy.

"Ooh-wee! That's that shit to put some hair on your chest right there!" he said, sucking his teeth and placing the glass down. "All right, Jordan. I don't know if this is the alcohol talking, but I think I have a solution for you. After kicking it with you today, I can tell that pushing this wedding back is something that you don't want to do. I can also tell that your job is very important to you. With that being said, I think I might be able to pull a few strings to get J-Net back where it needs to be."

"You don't have to do that," Jordan said, shaking his head. "There isn't anything anybody can do to help me now."

"Oh, but I do and I can. As you know, I work for a software company myself. A software company that is worth one hundred million as of this year. What if I told you that we could get you out of the hole?"

"Unless you have twenty million dollars lying around somewhere, I don't think you can help me."

"And what if I told you that we do? What if I told you that I could work out a deal to loan your company the money if you fulfill a small contract with us to make it back?"

"I would ask you, what's the catch?"

"We can iron out all of the details, of course, and once I get back to the office, I'll have the legal team contact you. But there is no catch. Just a brotha helping out another," Isaiah said, patting Jordan on the back. "But—"

"I knew it."

"Hear me out," Isaiah said and put his hands up to let Jordan know that he meant no harm. "The 'but' is that maybe you should keep this deal a secret from the old man for a while."

"And why would I do something like that?"

"Because some of the strings that I might have to pull to get you out of the hole may not be all the way ethical, for lack of a better term."

"So how do I explain a twenty-million-dollar hole being filled like that?"

"Don't," Isaiah said simply. "Tell him that if you are going to be taking care of the company one day, then he's going to need to trust you."

"You barely know me," Jordan stated. "Why would you stick your neck out like that for someone you just met?"

"I know that you mean something to the woman I love, and that says a lot because she doesn't really like anybody. That's all I need to know. So what do you say?"

Jordan looked as if he was pondering over Isaiah's words. The vein in his temple was showing, and he looked back to the dance floor at Lia. He finished off his Hennessy and set the glass down with a small nod.

"Have your legal team contact me, and if I like the terms, then we have ourselves a deal."

"Perfect! Problem solved. Now let's go find those women of ours."

The words were barely out of his mouth when suddenly there was a loud eruption of commotion. His eyes shot to the dance floor, and he was alarmed to see a fight going on. He was more surprised to see Lia and Matise at the center of it. It was four against two, and Lia and Matise seemed to have the upper hand. Isaiah saw security fighting against the big crowd of onlookers to get to the women, and he knew it was time to go before everyone in the place got pepper sprayed.

"What the hell?" Jordan yelled, and he too jumped into action.

They reached the women just as Lia was kicking a girl in the stomach and Matise socked another square in the jaw. Isaiah scooped up Lia while Jordan scooped Matise up, and they raced for the doors. They didn't stop until they were all safe in the car and pulling out of the parking lot.

"Yo, what the fuck was that?" Isaiah demanded, looking in his rearview mirror at the two women.

"That bitch bumped into her!" Lia yelled in a drunken slur. "She tried to punk my bitch!"

"Matise, you don't even fight!" Jordan said and turned to look at her incredulously.

"I avoid conflict," she corrected him. "But just because I don't like to fight doesn't mean I won't knock a bitch out for disrespecting me!"

"Did any of those women do anything else besides bump into you two?"

Lia and Matise looked at each other and fumbled with their words for a few moments before bursting into a fit of giggles. Those giggles turned into full-blown, stomach-clenching laughter.

"Y'all are crazy." Jordan shook his head. "I'm too drunk to deal with this shit right now."

"Tacos!" Matise yelled. "I want tacos! Take me to Abelardos!"

"What the hell is a Albrado?"

"Abe-lar-dos," Matise corrected her, cracking up. "It's food, bitch! I neeeed foooood!"

"Me toooooo!" Lia yelled and fell across Matise's lap. "I want tacos!"

Jordan looked at Isaiah with disbelieving eyes right before he too started to laugh. Isaiah, on the other hand, didn't find a thing funny. He was trying to hide it, but he was furious. He didn't know what Lia was playing at, but he was going to get to the bottom of it.

"I'm starting to feel the effects of that Hennessy, and I'm not trying to crash your whip," Isaiah said to Jordan. "So I'm going to just go back to your spot and hope you have something with some grease in that freezer."

"Bet," Jordan said, leaning back in his seat and closing his eyes.

Isaiah checked in the back seat. Lia and Matise were still laughing and talking about what had just happened in the club. He and Lia connected eyes, and for a second it seemed like she had sobered up, but only for a second. She rolled her eyes at him and continued talking to Matise. The more Isaiah watched her, the more he realized he'd never seen her like that before on the job. Normally she was disconnected from their hits and only showed them what she wanted them to see. She never let loose, and she did whatever she needed to do to get the job done. All she cared about was money, and Isaiah even believed she had a little fun luring people into her trap right before she pounced. She never caught feelings because that always made it easier to move on to the next.

At first, Isaiah felt bad for letting her in on all his schemes and scams. She'd already had such a tough life, but soon he saw that she liked it. She got off on all of the lying and the thieving. For him, it was about business, but for her it was pleasure. That was one of the reasons why she was the perfect accomplice. But right then, as he watched her, he recognized her. And that wasn't a good thing. She was being herself and letting her guard down. That worried him. He was starting to think that she was getting too attached to the job. He hoped that she wasn't playing with the idea of actually being Mrs. Heart, because from the way Jordan was talking, she was. And that couldn't happen because that job wasn't just about acquiring J-Net. It was personal.

Chapter 13

Lia

"Shit!" she exclaimed when she woke up the next morning.

The sun had just started to come up and was saying hello to her through the window curtains. She had sat up and tried to stretch her muscles, but an ache came that was so bad that she stopped mid-extend. The events from the night before came rushing back to her, and she suddenly remembered that she'd gotten into a fight. She didn't really recall why exactly she was mad. All that came to mind was how she felt. There was an anger that dwelled inside of her heart that she did well at keeping contained. But when she wasn't in the right state of mind, like last night when she was drinking, anything could set her off. She looked down at her swollen knuckles and cut her eyes when she saw her nails.

"Those bitches broke three of my nails." She sucked her teeth in annoyance.

Checking the digital clock next to the bed, she saw that it was only seven-thirty in the morning. It never mattered how late she went to sleep, she was always up earlier than she should have been. Her stomach growled, and she realized that she and Matise must have never gotten those tacos they were yelling about. She looked over to where Jordan was passed out, and she smiled at the sight of him sleeping with his mouth wide open. So as not to wake him, she climbed carefully out of the bed. Then she bounded downstairs to the kitchen.

"I need grease in my life," she groaned to herself and opened the freezer door. "Ding! Ding! Ding! Bacon for the win!"

She preheated the oven, because she preferred her bacon baked, and got a cookie sheet out of one of the cabinets. Once she set that on the counter by the oven, Lia went to one of the drawers in the island and pulled out a sheet of foil to lay down on the cookie sheet. The bacon would be done thawing by the time the oven sounded. The one thing Isaiah's mother had done while she was staying with them was teach Lia her way around the kitchen. That was, of course, before her husband began making his way in her room at night.

As she waited for the oven to get done warming up, she thought about how much she loved cooking for Jordan. She'd been slowly but surely spending more time at his home than hers even though she knew that was a bad idea. She was really starting to get comfortable with the idea of seriously becoming Mrs. Lia Heart. She'd been working with Isaiah for so long, and at first, she never saw the end of it, mainly because she never thought of it. She never really thought about her future before. She had always been an "in the moment" person. Things were different with Jordan. Maybe, after Isaiah got what he wanted, she could continue being the Lia everyone loved. After Isaiah broke Matise's heart, she could be the friend to fly out to her and console her. Maybe she could throw away the malicious, conniving woman she'd been for so long and settle down to have a normal life.

"Jordan and Lia Heart," she said out loud and smiled at the sound of it. "I now pronounce you husband and wife."

She wrapped her arms around herself and closed her eyes. She envisioned the ballroom exactly how she and

Matise mapped it out, and she pretended to be dancing with Jordan. She swayed her body all around the kitchen, humming a sweet tune of love before she was interrupted by the sound of someone clearing their throat.

"Am I interrupting something?"

Lia twisted her head around to see who had caught her in her moment of bliss and found Isaiah standing at the entrance of the kitchen. He was wearing a T-shirt and a pair of checkered gray and black pajama bottoms. He took a few steps toward her while looking around the elegant room, and his eyes stopped on the burgundy accent wall. They lingered for a second before he looked back to Lia. She put her hand on her hip and cocked her head, wondering what the hint of a smile on his lips was for.

"What?"

"Isn't burgundy your favorite color?"

"Yes, and?" She jerked her head slightly like she had an attitude.

"I've just been noticing all of your little add-ons and touches around the house, that's all. You seem comfortable."

"Is that a problem?"

"Hmm," he said and circled around her. "You're really doing a hell of a job with the performance this time."

"Isn't that the point?"

"I would say yes, but you're doing too well of a job. You even almost had me convinced last night. Starting a bar fight because someone disrespected your 'bitch,' as you put it. And you and Jordan seem really cozy."

"If you're trying to say something then say it," Lia said in a low tone and glared at him.

"Are you getting attached?"

"No."

"Are you sure about that?" he said and stopped circling around Lia when he was directly in front of her. "Are you sure you aren't falling in love with him? For real, and not for pretend?"

"I . . . I—"

Beep!

The loud signal from the oven went off, telling her that it was done preheating, and she turned her back to him. She grabbed the bacon out of the water in the sink and started spreading the strips out on the cookie sheet once she opened the pack. She felt Isaiah boring a hole in the back of her head with his eyes. If he weren't her cousin, she would throw a meat clever at his face with no remorse.

"You do know that this isn't real, right? You know that he doesn't love you, right? He loves the person you're pretending to be."

The way he said the word "pretending" made her heart skip a beat. Lia bit the inside of her cheek and held her composure. She wasn't going to let him know that his words had gotten to her.

"You don't have to worry about me," she said, turning her head slightly. "You just worry about your payback. It's looking like you and Matise are getting closer as well. You like her, I can tell."

"I like her," Isaiah admitted, "but I love me. You asked me to keep her busy while you work your magic and charm him into expanding his business with NYC Partners. Well, now there is a change of plans. Because of your little stunt with Bancroft, Jacob Heart was not going to sign over the company to Jordan. It seems like J-Net has a bit of debt that Daddy doesn't want to pass on to his son. That would have ruined everything, so I had to show my hand to fix it."

"What did you do?" Lia asked, shocked by his revelation.

"Instead of acquiring J-Net, I have decided to strike an ongoing business deal with them. I told Jordan that it would just be temporary, but I'm sure he'll want to stay on board. Especially after you break the news to him."

"Break what news to him?"

"That you can't marry him and that you're moving away. He will be so confused and heartbroken that he will want to bury himself in work. My work."

"W . . . what?"

"I don't need you anymore for this, Lia. I will still pay you what we agreed upon once you get back to New York. I will give you until next week to tell Jordan the news. You have become a conflict of interest, and I can't risk it."

"So you expect me to cut things off with Jordan while you live happily ever after with Matise?" Lia asked in awe.

"That will soon come to an end too. Unlike you, I didn't catch feelings."

Lia felt like a hammer was trying to bash through her chest and get to her heart. Her breathing had become shallow, and she turned the rest of her body away from him. She didn't say anything to him for a moment. Instead, she put the cookie sheet in the oven and washed her hands, trying to contain her emotions.

"This," she started, motioning all around the house with one of her hands, "has been my life for almost a year now. This is my . . . this is my home."

"This is not your home, Lia."

"Well, why can't it be? Why can't I have my happily ever after?"

"Because it isn't real!" he exclaimed in a hushed tone. "You are not Lia Blackstone who was raised in some orphanage in Texas like you told Jordan. You are Malia Trenton. The same Malia Trenton who set her own home on fire with her parents inside because they made you see a shrink three times a week. The same Malia Trenton who helped me kill my parents for hurting you. You are not the person you are pretending to be."

"But I can be," she whispered. "That's in my past. I'm a changed person now. I just want to be happy."

"If I let you stay, sooner or later they're going to find out who you really are. And I can't have that. I should have never involved you in any of this, but we've never had this problem before. I hired you to be a distraction, not to fall in love. You've become a liability, Lia. If Jordan somehow finds out what you did with that Bancroft deal, it would be the end of the company."

"He won't find out!"

"Don't be so sure." Isaiah shook his head and sighed. "Once Jordan agrees to my offer, and he will, don't you think he'll be doing business with Bancroft? What do you think will happen when their CEO sees that Jordan's wife is the same person who blackmailed him into signing a contract with me? It would blow up in our faces and ruin everything that I have ever worked for, and that is just something that I won't allow. So you will do as I told you and break things off with Jordan, do you understand?"

Lia glared at him again and whipped around in anger. She leaned forward, gripping the counter so tight that she almost broke every nail that wasn't already. Behind her, she heard him move and grab something off the counter, but before she could look and see what it was, he had already snatched her head back by her hair.

"I said do you understand?" he repeated, pressing a sharp knife against her neck.

"I understand," she said in an angry breath. "Now move this knife from my neck if you aren't going to use it."

He waited a few seconds before he let her go and put the knife back. Her fingers flew to where it had been on her neck, and when she withdrew them, she saw tiny specks of blood. She stared at them until her vision blurred, not believing that Isaiah was the source of it. But he was.

"I'm going back to bed before Matise notices that I'm missing. I have to meet her parents later today, so you two can have one last girls' day pretending to map out the wedding. But I expect you to be gone by next week. I'll have the money transferred into your account."

Her back was still to him when she heard his feet walking out of the kitchen, but there was one thing that she wanted to say to him before he was gone.

"I know the real reason why you switched the target from his father to Jordan," she whispered just loud enough for him to hear. "I know the real reason why you want to hurt him so bad."

She heard Isaiah's feet stop, but only for a split second. He kept going without saying anything else to Lia, leaving her dismal and full of emotions. The last time she felt like that she burned her own house down. The smell of bacon snapped her out of her trance, and she came to a sound conclusion. If Isaiah thought that she was going to leave Jordan, he had another think coming. She was going to be Mrs. Jordan Heart whether he liked it or not.

Chapter 14

Matise

I spun around like a girl from a movie and let the skirt to the dress I had on fly. It was a beautiful floral Dolce & Gabbana dress with thick straps and a square neckline that I couldn't help but try on. It wasn't what I had come for. I was supposed to be finding a purse to match my dress for the wedding. Jordan wanted me as his best man—well, woman—but because I refused to wear a suit, Lia said that it would be okay if I was her maid of honor since she didn't really have any close friends. Jordan chose his closest cousin, Trent, to be his best man instead, and everything worked out. While I was there, Lia and I had gotten a lot accomplished. At first, she wanted to wear Mrs. Heart's wedding dress, but we both agreed that she needed something that was more "her." Not only did we find the most beautiful dress for her, but we found the most perfect dresses for me and the bridesmaids.

I had to admit that I had truly enjoyed myself and was happy that I'd gotten a chance to get to know who Lia was. Hearing about how hard her life had been growing up going from home to home made me kind of happy that she finally found happiness, even if it was with Jordan. When shopping, I told Amara about the club fight we'd gotten into, she couldn't believe it.

"You got into a fight?" she asked in a disbelieving tone. "Miss I Don't Like Confrontation?"

She was sitting pretty in a large, cushioned chair wearing a cute mustard-colored jumpsuit and a pair of white pumps. She patiently was watching me look at myself in the mirror like any good friend would do. I'd asked her to come look at a few things with me after work, and she agreed since we hadn't spent much time together outside of work in the week since I'd been back.

"Yes, I did, and it was so much fun!" I admitted while checking out my profile in the dress.

"What!"

"I know it sounds crazy, but I just don't remember the last time I felt so alive!"

"So you mean to tell me beating up people makes you happy? Let me remember to stay on your good side!"

"No," I giggled. "I hated the beating people up part. But the rush of it all just reminded me of how much life I've been missing out on. All I've been doing lately is working and being grumpy. It has taken so much of my energy, so that weekend was a much-needed one."

"Well, I'm happy you enjoyed yourself. How did your parents feel about Isaiah?"

"They liked him I guess." I shrugged. "But you've met my dad. He doesn't think anyone is good enough for his baby girl. He played nice though. I think he only did it for me."

"I'm sure he and your mom had a conversation about him when y'all left."

"Girl, I'm sure of it too! Hell, it was out of nowhere after all."

I went back to the dressing room to take the dress off. I liked it a lot, but not enough to buy it. Plus, that's not what I came for. I hurried to put my lavender dress, white blazer, and white peep-toe heels back on so that Amara and I could go look at purses. The dress that she'd chosen for my dress was burgundy, and I hoped to find a cream-colored purse to wear with it. Not too big, but not something that was super tiny either. As I was walking around the store picking up bags and putting them back down, I noticed Amara looking at me funny.

"What?" I asked and touched my face before digging in my lavender clutch to find my mirror. "I know you're not letting me walk around looking crazy!"

"No, you look fine, really."

"Then why are you looking at me like that?"

"Because you're in this store looking for a bag to wear to Lia's wedding, that's why. How do you feel about being her maid of honor?"

"What do you mean?" I asked and made a face. "How am I supposed to feel?"

"I don't know. Don't you think it's a little weird?"

"No. Why would I?"

"Um, gee, I don't know, because you hated her guts a month ago?"

"I did not hate her!" I laughed. "I just didn't trust her."

"And you trust her now?"

"Yeah, she's a good girl."

"Why doesn't she have any of her own friends in her wedding? Didn't you say her bridesmaids are Jordan's cousins?"

"She had a tough life, and that made it really hard for her to get close to anyone."

"Uh-huh," Amara said, sucking her teeth. "Okay. Well, don't you think it's a little awkward for you to be her maid of honor when you were just madly in love with her fiancé?"

"Oh my God!" I exclaimed and set the purse that I was looking at back down. "I am not doing this with you right now! I invited you here to be supportive, not get on my damn nerves with twenty-one questions."

"You're going to need my support all right when you see how fine Jordan looks in that tux and you're playing besties with his wife-to-be," she said and ducked out of the way before I could pop her.

"Keep playing with me, hear?" I warned with my finger pointed at her.

"I'm just saying," Amara said, putting her hands up. "Just want to make sure you're really okay with all of this."

"I am," I said in a convincing tone, even though I did feel a small dip at the bottom of my stomach.

She studied me for a few more moments before letting me off the hook. She grabbed a cute cognac tote bag and held it up to me. It was cute, but not what I was looking for.

"I was thinking something smaller," I said, making a face.

"Girl, this wasn't for you! I have the perfect shoes to match this!" she said, clutching the bag to her chest. "Anyways, how are you and Mr. Dreamy?"

"Who, Isaiah?"

"You say that like you have multiples." Amara raised her eyebrows at me. "Do you?"

"No, silly. We're good. I'm actually going to dinner with him later tonight."

"Well you guys have been going strong, haven't you?"

"You can say that. I haven't seen him in a few days though. I hope meeting my parents didn't run him off, you know?"

"Girl, if that man rode your cold-ass wave for months before you actually gave him the time of day, nothing can scare him off."

"True. I've been wondering where this thing between us is going, you know?"

"Oh shit!" Amara exclaimed in a hushed tone. Her mouth was formed in an "O," and she was smiling at me with her eyes. "Let me find out you're thinking about a serious commitment."

"You are so dramatic!" I rolled my eyes. "But yes, I have been thinking about it. I think it's time I try this whole boyfriend-girlfriend thing out and see where it takes me."

"Have you talked to him about it?"

"No, but I was going to tonight. He's supposed to be coming over with Chinese."

"Mmm. Your favorite."

"I know, isn't he so dreamy," I said, mocking her.

"I can't stand you sometimes," she said and pretended to hit me with a bag. "Let me stop before one of these white ladies thinks I'm trying to steal this thing."

We laughed and talked for the next thirty minutes. That's how long it took me to find the perfect purse, but it was worth the search. By the time we left the store, it was just about to be seven o'clock in the evening. We bid each other farewell and said we would see each other at work. The moment I started driving in the direction of my home, my phone began ringing through the Bluetooth of my car.

"Hello?" I said after I clicked the answer button on my steering wheel.

"Boo, I miss you!"

I smiled when I heard Lia's voice. "I know! But I'll be back soon. Did you get my e-mail with all of the stuff we need to order?"

"Girl, yes, and Jordan just about had a damn cow when he saw the price. What are you trying to do? Make me get divorced before I even get married?"

"Jordan will be all right! Tell him to just give you the damn credit card," I said, and I heard her laugh come through my speakers.

"What do you think I did? I am going to have my dream wedding whether he likes it or not! But anyways, what are you up to?"

"Nothing, about to go home. Isaiah is supposed to be coming over to feed me."

After I said that the line got real quiet. I turned the volume up in my car just in case it was because I'd just hopped on the highway, but that didn't change anything. I still couldn't hear her.

"Lia, are you still there?"

"I'm sorry, girl, I got lost in my own head for a second. What did you say?"

"It's okay, honey. I just said Isaiah is going to stop by later."

"You guys are still dating?"

"Um, yeah. It's only been a week since we were there."

"I know, it's just I guess I didn't get that lovey-dovey vibe from him."

"Really?"

"Yeah. Don't get me wrong, he seems like a really sweet guy. I don't know. He just gave me the vibe of a lustful man. I didn't want to say anything at the time because I didn't want to kill the mood, but I swear I saw him get a number at the club."

"Wow," I said, shaking my head. "Are you serious? Now that I think about it, I swear I felt him get out of bed with me right after we got home that night. I thought I was just dreaming though. Do you think . . . do you think he left and went somewhere?"

"Te Te, I'm going to say it just like this. Trust men as far as you can throw them. You can't put anything past anybody."

"Even Jordan?"

"Jordan is different," she said and then laughed. "I don't know how. He just is."

"Uh-huh," I said. Her words were weighing heavy on my mind. There I was planning to tell Isaiah that I was ready to take the thing between us up another notch, and then I find out something like that. Maybe Lia calling me was a sign to just keep my mouth shut.

"I'm sorry, Te Te," she said and genuinely sounded sorry. "I just can tell that you were really feeling him. I don't want my girl to be out here looking dumb behind some man who thinks he can do whatever he wants. Men with good jobs are always like that."

"Tell me about it. What's done in the dark always comes to the light."

"Yeah, it does. Well, I was just calling to tell you that I miss you. Even though I told you yesterday."

"And the day before," I reminded her.

"Because you're my girl!" she said. "I'll call you tomorrow. Good luck with Mr. CEO."

"He's the one who's going to need it, not me."

We disconnected the phone, and I got lost in my thoughts until I was pulling into my parking garage. Could what Lia told me be true? I mean, we were all pretty drunk that night, but why would she tell me something like that if it weren't true? She didn't have any reason to lie to me. I was so overcome with the things going through my head that I didn't know how I ended up in my living room on the couch. I didn't even remember getting out of my car. The more I recalled that night, the more I distinctively remembered Isaiah getting out of bed when he thought I was asleep.

Since I was younger, I had always been a firecracker. I shot first and asked questions later because I hated when people made me angry. And that's the feeling that I was getting to. Did he really leave the bed we were in to go lie up with some hoochie? A sweaty-ass ho he'd met in the club he was at with me? The more I thought about it, the more I needed to know the truth. And I needed to know before he showed up at my door, trying to come in and slide between my legs. I pulled my phone out of my clutch and kicked my heels off to get comfortable. I dialed his number, and it rang four times before I heard his deep voice answer.

"I was just about to call you," he said, and I heard the smile in his voice. "I know you always get combination fried rice, but tonight I thought maybe you wanted to do something different."

"Kind of like you wanted to do something different?" I didn't mean to just blurt it out like that, but I did so oh well.

"What?" he asked, sounding puzzled.

"You heard me," I said. "I was just on the phone with Lia talking about the wedding, and she told me that she saw you get a girl's number at the club."

"She said what?"

"You heard me! Say 'what' again and I'm going to curse you out!" I exclaimed. "Is it true?"

"Are you serious right now?"

"I'm dead-ass serious." I sighed and looked up at the ceiling. "You know, I understand that we aren't a full-fledged couple yet, so I can't really get mad about you talking to someone else. I'm mad because it was in my hometown."

"Matise, I don't know what lies Lia told you, but I didn't get anyone's number that night at the club. Jordan and I were talking business."

"Oh please!" I said in disbelief. "That's your cover-up?"

"It can't be a cover-up if it's the truth."

"Okay, so where did you go that night?"

"What?"

"Didn't I just tell you if you said that damn word one more time, I was going to curse your lying, sorry ass out? I saw you get out of the bed, Isaiah! It had to have been three in the morning. Where did you go?"

Silence.

"Hellooo? Am I talking to myself?"

"Matise . . ."

"Where did you go, Isaiah?"

"I can't tell you that, but it isn't what you think."

"Yeah," I said, feeling my heart sink inside of my chest. "I bet it wasn't."

"Mati—"

"Save it," I tried to snap, but my voice broke. "Just save it okay? And don't come by here tonight or ever again. I don't want anything to do with a man who lies to me."

I hung up the phone and tossed it to the other side of the couch. I had to take a few deep breaths to calm myself down. Was that how it felt to have your heart broken? I felt sick to my stomach, and I just wanted to lie down, so I did. I didn't care about the fact that I was still fully dressed, or the fact that the sun was still out. I buried my head in my pillow and cried my eyes out. I cried because right when I thought I had finally found balance in my life, the scale teetered. I cried because I felt like a fool. I cried because my best friend was moving on to the next phase in his life without me. And lastly, I cried because I had never felt so alone in my life.

Chapter 15

Isaiah

"Matise!" Isaiah yelled into the phone, but it was no use. She'd already disconnected the line. "Shit!"

His sudden outburst made everyone in the Chinese restaurant give him funny stares. He cancelled his entire order and left to go get back in his car. After he used all his force to shut the door, he slammed his back into the seat and tugged his tie loose. He contemplated going to Matise's house anyway but thought better of it. He could hear in her voice how hurt she was, and he knew she wouldn't even open the door. He didn't know why he wanted to go and console her so badly, especially when he was supposed to be cutting her loose. He wanted her to know that she had the wrong idea completely. However, he couldn't. If he did that, then he would have to tell her where he really was, and he couldn't do that either. He could only think of one thing to do: call Lia.

"What the fuck is wrong with you!" he shouted the moment he heard the line open up. "Why would you tell Matise some messed-up stuff like that?"

"Damn, that was faster than I thought," she snickered. "I was just messing with her. I didn't think she would actually believe me."

"Bullshit," he sneered. "And I thought I told you to break it off with Jordan."

"Yeah, see, I thought about it, I really did. But then I realized how unfair it would be if I had to cut Jordan off and you didn't have to do the same with Matise."

"I told you why you have to end things with Jordan. He just sent over the signed documents today! It's not the same."

"How isn't it? I'm not letting him go, and you can't make me. Not even if you put another knife to my neck."

"Listen to yourself. You sound ridiculous."

"Do I really? Why can't we both get what we want? You know you love her, Isaiah. Everybody loves Matise!"

"Yeah, but not as much as you, huh?"

"And what is that supposed to mean? Hello? What do you mean by that?"

Click.

He knew there was no point going back and forth with her. Lia had gotten to a point of no return, so there were no words he could say to bring her back to reality. He was almost positive that she didn't even live in reality. He was really starting to believe that she thought she truly was the person she'd been pretending to be. Some part of her really thought that she could have a happily ever after, because before then, she never went against his orders.

The words she'd said to him in Jordan's kitchen kept ringing over and over in his head.

I know the real reason why you switched the target from his father to Jordan. I know the real reason why you want to hurt him so bad.

But she couldn't have. It just wasn't possible. Unless she'd found out some other way that he couldn't think of. There were some things he'd kept her in the dark about when he recruited her for the J-Net mission. Like that he'd visited Nebraska before he even called her about the job.

Isaiah had never been as nervous about anything as he was sitting in the lobby of his competitor. He'd sat in his car for twenty minutes, giving himself a pep talk before he had even made his way inside of the company. Many people were bustling around trying to get to where they needed to be and didn't pay him any mind. Good, he liked it that way. He fixed the diamond cuff links on his black suit and made sure his cherry red tie was on straight when the secretary finally told him that it was time to go back. She was a cute black woman, short but thick. Her hair was cut in a pixie cut, and she had make-up caked on her face.

"I like your dress," he said, complimenting the long, formfitting midnight blue dress. "It accents your physique perfectly."

"Why, thank you," she said, smiling at him as she led him down a few long hallways. "Don't tell anyone, but I wore it to a job interview earlier today. And it might be the reason why they offered me the job!"

"Maybe so," Isaiah said, chuckling.

"I start next month, so I guess I'll have to tell the boss soon. They'll have to start looking for someone to replace me."

"Well, I'm sure they'll miss you."

"I'm sure they will too, Mr. Partners," she said and stopped at a wide door and held her arm out. "Well, here we are. Mr. Heart is expecting you. If you need anything on the way out, please let me know."

She turned on her heels and power-walked back to her desk in the lobby, leaving him alone outside of the closed door. Isaiah smoothed out the jacket of his suit and fixed his tie one more time before knocking twice on the door.

"Come in!" a deep, husky voice called.

When Isaiah opened the door, he saw a man sitting at a large desk in his huge office. He was on the phone, but he waved for Isaiah to come in and have a seat. Isaiah closed the door behind him and sat down in the seat on the other side of the desk. Mr. Heart held up a finger as if to tell him that it would just be another second.

"Yes, I understand, Jordan. But what about revenue?" he said into the phone and then paused. "Well all right, I'm trusting you on this one. But listen, I have someone in my office. I'll stop by your door before I leave today." He disconnected the phone and gave Isaiah a big smile and held out his hand. "Sorry. My son and his crazy ideas! You must be Isaiah Partners, owner of NYC Partners! I've heard remarkable things about your company, young man!"

"Thank you, Mr. Heart," Isaiah said and shook his hand. "I appreciate you taking this meeting on such short notice."

"No problem at all. To what do I owe this pleasure? One can only assume that you aren't here to just sight-see."

"Straight to business, I like that." Isaiah smiled. "Well, to make a long story short, a little birdie told me that you were looking into a merger deal."

"Is that right?" Mr. Heart looked at Isaiah curiously. "A little birdie like who?"

"Come on, Mr. Heart," Isaiah said in a playful tone. "You know this industry isn't quiet. There are a lot of things that slip through the cracks. Now this merger deal."

"What about it?"

"The little birdie told me that it is one that would take the industry by storm, and I'm here to make my offer."

"Your offer?" Mr. Heart said and furrowed his brow at Isaiah. "Your offer on what?"

"J-Net."

Mr. Heart looked at Isaiah as if he were joking. When it was apparent that he was dead serious, Mr. Heart let out a laugh that came from deep in his stomach. "My boy, you say that like we are for sale."

"Everybody has a price. You haven't even heard my offer yet."

"Like I said," Mr. Heart said, staring intently at Isaiah, "we aren't for sale. The only thing open for a deal is a merger between two companies. That is all that is on the table for now, and if it is something you want to discuss, then I'm all ears. If not, then I don't know what to tell you, Mr. Partners."

"I'm sorry to hear that."

"Don't be. You're not the first person to walk through those doors and try to get me to sell my company, and you won't be the last. So, I'll tell you like I told all the others. A man's job is to build something that he can pass down to his children, and J-Net is my something, understand? When the time comes, I will step down from my seat and pass this company down to my son."

"Your son, huh?" Isaiah chuckled. "Which one?"

Isaiah matched Mr. Heart's glare in its entirety. They both had the same brown eyes that slanted ever so slightly in the corners. Both of their foreheads crinkled up the exact same way when upset, and their noses were flared.

"I only have one son," Mr. Heart said.

"Are you so sure about that? Or is that just what you want to believe, Jacob?"

"Believe? I know! I don't know who you think I am, young man, but I can assure you that I'm not him."

"Karen Partners," Isaiah said loudly. "Well, thirty years ago it was Karen Seals. You two were high-school sweethearts. She got pregnant."

"No." Mr. Heart shook his head in disbelief. He stood up and began to pace the room, rubbing a hand across the top of his head. It looked like everything was coming back to him. "That's not possible. She . . . she—"

"Was pregnant."

"No, I know she was pregnant." Mr. Heart stopped pacing to lean with his hands on the top of his desk. "I gave her the money to get rid of you. I heard that she had a little boy sometime later, but by then she was married."

"He wasn't my father."

"And how do you know that?"

"Because she told me before she died. And I can guarantee that if I take a DNA test, I would be a perfect match to you. And I think you know it, too."

Mr. Heart studied Isaiah's face, and realization washed all over his own. He slowly slid back down into his own seat and stroked the hairs on his chin. He was so deep in thought that the vein on his temple was throbbing.

"What is it that you want?" he asked.

"My rightful place in your empire. I am your firstborn son. Look at me. Just look at what I've built on my own! I am more than competent to—"

"I can't risk this getting out to the public," Mr. Heart cut him off before he finished his sentence. He put his hands up in the air and shook his head hard. "The world can never know about a mistake that was made years ago. My family, my colleagues . . . I'm not going to let you come in here and ruin everything that I've built!"

"Ruin? I'm your son!"

"No, you are a grown-ass man I have never seen in my life."

"Look in the mirror! You see me every day!" Isaiah said and jumped up from his seat.

"How much to make you go away?" Mr. Heart asked.

"Are you serious?" Isaiah stared at him, astounded.

"Yes. I have my checkbook right here." Mr. Heart pulled a small booklet from one of the drawers in his desk. "Name your price."

"I have millions! I don't need your hush money. What I needed was a father!"

"Well, I already have a son."

His response set off a chain reaction of emotions inside of Isaiah. He frowned at the older man in disgust. He'd hoped that Jacob Heart would be a good man and own up to his mistakes, but that was too much like right for someone who was stuck in his ways. He locked eyes with his biological father one more time before he spoke in a low, menacing voice.

"Because you are too proud, this company and everything else you love are going to suffer. I promise you that."

"Get out of my office," Mr. Heart growled. "At once!"

"You don't have to tell me twice. Bye, Dad."

Isaiah came back to himself and noticed that he'd clenched his jaw tight while he was replaying the scene in his head. Lia couldn't have known that Jacob Heart was his father, but even if she did, that was okay. He knew a secret of hers, too, one he was going to use to get what he wanted.

It was a fact that Isaiah had indeed snuck out of the house while Matise was asleep, but it wasn't to go and have sex with another woman. There was something up with Lia that he couldn't put his finger on, and he planned on getting to the bottom of it. She was herself, but there was something different about her personality. Something different, but familiar. While everyone else in the house was passed out drunk, or so he thought, he took Lia's keys and hopped in Jordan's car. He drove to Lia's apartment, the one he'd accommodated her with, and went inside. He didn't know what he expected to find, but it definitely wasn't what he found. Deep in the back of her closet, there were at least fifteen pictures of Matise on the wall with a big one in the middle. That one looked a little worn compared to the others. Around all of the pictures, there were character traits and even phrases that he'd heard Matise say multiple times. There were even notes on wardrobe tips and what Matise's most common hairstyles were. Above all those things were two words: "my girl." He knew then that she wasn't just trying to keep Matise happy for Jordan's sake. She was so worried about it because she was obsessed with her. So obsessed that she didn't just want to be like Matise. It seemed as if she wanted to *be* her. He also realized another thing. If Lia was trying to become Matise, then it wasn't Lia who Jordan loved. It was Matise.

It was time for him to take matters into his own hands, and before he drove away, Isaiah reached into the glove compartment of his Mercedes. Inside there was a small burner phone, one that couldn't be traced back to him. Since Lia didn't want to leave Jordan alone, Isaiah would have to force his hand.

Everything isn't all that it seems. Want to know who your fiancée really is? Go to her house and look in her closet.

He sent the message as soon as he was done writing it. It didn't take long for the phone to give a strong vibrate in his hand when Jordan texted back.

Who is this?

Isaiah mulled over the question. Who was he?

A friend.

He sent the message, turned the phone off, and put it back in the glove compartment. He hoped the seed he'd planted would grow into a whole tree, but he would see. In the meantime, he needed to figure out what he was going to do about Matise. Maybe it was a good thing, them being over. Still, he hated that it wasn't on his terms. He didn't want them to end with her being mad at him, but why? No matter what way they ended, he didn't see it being on good terms. He'd heard her voice crack, and he'd be lying if he said he didn't feel that. He did, and suddenly he was questioning if he truly had fallen in love with her. There was just something special about her. It was something that you didn't find too often. Could he really let her go? To be truthful, the answer to that question was no. However, if he continued seeing her, he was sure Lia would do something to sabotage it again in her anger. She might even tell Lia who and what he really was, and he didn't want that. In the end, he decided that it was best that he leave her alone. He'd been presented with the opportunity to be done. No matter how far from ideal it was, it was something that just had to be.

Chapter 16

Jordan

A content feeling had completely taken over Jordan because everything in his life was structured. He didn't have to worry about crazy things like his tires being slashed or deciding who he was going to spend another loveless evening with. No, he sure didn't. Not now that he had the woman of his dreams. He peeked down at her in the dark movie theater. She had her head leaned comfortably on his chest as they sat close together watching the latest movie in the Marvel franchise. His arm was wrapped securely around her shoulders, and he gave her a small squeeze. She looked up at him and smiled.

"I love you," he whispered down at her.

"I love you too," she replied and accepted his sweet kiss before turning back to the movie.

It was pure bliss, the feeling of being in love was. It was a feeling he never thought would be returned to him. In the past, women would claim they loved him but only really be interested in what he could do for them. Or how he could advance their lives. What some women didn't understand was that men had feelings too. Yes, it was a man's job to take care of his woman and all of her needs. That's how Jordan was raised anyway. His father always told him that if he could not finance the dating process, then he should not be dating. No woman should ever lift a finger to even touch a bill if she had a good man in her corner. If a man had done all that he was supposed to do in life, then he should never expect things to be fifty-fifty with a woman. When he was young, Jordan's father told him that if a woman worked, her money was her money. But the man's money was their money.

"Good women take care of our children and teach them how to be good people while we are at work. They cook for us, wash our dirty drawers, and sleep with us whenever we get a rise in our pants. They take on every emotional burden that gets hurled our way so that we can get a full night's sleep, and they still get up at six in the morning to have breakfast ready and waiting on the table. They do all of this wanting only two things in return, love and loyalty. Those things are free. And because of that, all of your financial resources should be at their disposal."

The part that he left out, however, was that the woman's job was to just let him be a man, not brag to her friends about all that her man did for her. Jordan had been raised with respect and manners, but before he met Lia, that side of him was always ignored. It didn't matter how he treated women. He could be the biggest dog, and they would have stayed because of what he could do for them. In him they only saw dollar signs and opportunities, but not Lia. She saw him for the person he was inside and took the time to get to know who he really was. At first, when he met her, he thought that she was too good to be true. But throughout it all, she never changed once, and that's why he had fallen in love with her. That was why he asked her to be his wife.

Sometime toward the end of the movie, Jordan got the overwhelming sensation that he had to use the restroom. He didn't want to miss the movie since it was at the good part, and he tried to hold it. It got to the point where he just couldn't anymore. The way his bladder was set up, if he didn't go soon, it might explode.

"Excuse me, babe," he whispered and removed his arm.

"You okay?" she asked and leaned away from him.

"Yeah, I just need to run to the restroom."

"Okay, well hurry up! You're going to miss all of the good parts."

He kissed her forehead before he stood up. It had been Lia's idea to sit at two of the end row seats, and that had been smart thinking because he didn't mess up anyone's view as he made his way out of the AMC theater. He rushed to the restroom, and once he was inside, he emptied his entire bladder into one of the urinals.

"Ahhh," he said as he relieved himself. "I shouldn't have drunk all of that damn pop."

When he was done, he washed his hands and was about to go back to his seat when his phone vibrated in his pocket. Thinking it was Lia telling him to go grab something from concessions, he pulled it out of the pocket of his jeans. The number displayed across the screen was one that he didn't recognize it, and he almost didn't open it. Almost.

Everything isn't all that it seems. Want to know who your fiancée really is? Go to her house and look in her closet.

He read and reread the message, trying to make sense of it. One, he didn't know how the person had gotten his number. And two, what did they mean by who Lia really was? He crinkled his brow and asked the person who they were.

A friend.

Jordan didn't like the message that he received back, and he'd had enough of playing around. He tried to call the number, but it kept going to one of those automated voicemails, and it didn't say a name. He stared at his phone for a few moments longer before shaking it off. It was probably just someone playing on his phone. He put it back in his pocket and went back to the movie.

"Took you long enough," Lia joked when he took his seat.

"Yeah," Jordan said, trying to act normal. "My bad."

"You okay? I thought you fell in or something."

"Yeah, I'm good," Jordan said and held his arm up so that she could lie back on him. "What'd I miss?"

"A lot of action."

She went back to watching the movie, and Jordan did his best to stay focused on the film too, but his brain began to work overtime. He couldn't stop thinking about the strange message, and he wondered who sent it. Did the person mean "closet" literally or figuratively? Not only that, but up until then he never paid attention to the fact that he had never even really gone to Lia's place. There was no point since she was always at his. He glanced down at her and wondered if she was hiding something from him. She'd never given him a reason to think that she was, but still . . .

When the movie was over, Jordan could honestly say that he had no idea what happened in the end. He had been too consumed by his own curiosity. It was almost nine o'clock at night when they left the theater to go to his house. In the car on the way, he took his phone out and looked at the messages again as he drove.

"Who is that?" Lia asked and tried to peek at the screen.

"Nobody," Jordan said and closed out of his message app.

"Mm-hmm," she said, lowering her eyes at him. "Jordan Heart, if you are texting another woman I will kill you."

"It wasn't another woman."

"If you say so. Can you stop by the gas station, please? All that popcorn has my mouth dry as hell, and that pop didn't make it any better."

"Sure," he said.

He stopped at the first gas station he came across and parked. He always kept a twenty-dollar bill in his armrest, and he got it out to give it to her for whatever she was going to get.

"Thank you, baby. Did you want anything?"

"No, I'm good," Jordan told her with a smile.

"Okay, I'll be right back."

She got out of the car, and he watched her switch into the gas station. She got a few catcalls, but it didn't bother him. She was looking pretty thick in her jeans, after all. When she was completely gone and inside of the gas station, Jordan looked in her seat and saw that she'd left her purse. Sitting right on top of her wallet were her keys, and he went to grab them, but he stopped himself.

"You're tripping, man," he said out loud to himself. "She isn't hiding anything from you."

As much as he wanted to believe his own words, he couldn't remove the doubt from the back of his mind. He looked to make sure she wasn't coming back out yet before he reached and took the keys out of the purse. He put them in the armrest and hoped she didn't notice them missing when she came back out. A few minutes later the passenger door opened, and Lia got back in the car with a slushy and a hot dog with nothing but mustard on top.

"I don't know why, but gas station dogs are the best!" she exclaimed and took a big bite out of it. "Mmm! You want some?" She held the hot dog to his mouth, but he shook his head no.

"I'm good. I'll probably just grab something to eat later."

"I can make you something when we get to the house," she offered. "What do you feel like eating?"

"No, that's okay," he said, focusing his eyes on the road.

It only took them fifteen minutes to get home since there wasn't much traffic on the street that night. When he pulled into the driveway, he hit the button for the garage to open, but he didn't pull in. Lia looked at him with questioning eyes.

"You're not going to pull in?"

"I was just dropping you off. My dad just called not too long ago. He needs me to stop into the office to grab some paperwork really fast."

"Oh well, I can just come with you," she suggested.

"Nah, we're already home. You go ahead and go in, and I'll be back in a few."

"Well oookayyy," she told him and opened her door to get out. "I love you, and I'll see you when you get back. When you go by my desk will you bring me my favorite purple pen? That's a good pen, and I don't want Jen's thieving ass to take it."

"Will do," he said and kissed her on the cheek. "I'll see you in a little bit."

Jordan waited for her to gather her things and shut the door. He made sure that she was safely inside of the house and that the garage door was closed all the way before he drove away. As he went in the direction of Lia's home, he felt that he was being crazy and insecure. He was going based off what a ghost had told him about his woman, and in all honesty, the person hadn't even told him anything. Yet, he couldn't rest until he got the nagging feeling of doubt out of his brain. He hoped that Lia wouldn't notice that her house keys were missing before he had a chance to return them.

He pulled into the parking lot of the apartment complex and parked a little way away from the entrance to Lia's building. Jordan turned the engine of his car off and checked his surroundings to make sure no one was around watching him. For all he knew, it could have been a setup. When all he saw was an older Mexican man outside on his patio smoking a cigarette and the apartment security vehicle making its rounds, he figured the coast was clear.

He got out and bounded toward the door and used the keys to open the secured entry. As he went up the three flights of carpeted stairs, he took in the smell of laundry detergent and dryer sheets and assumed someone must have been doing laundry in the basement of the building. When he finally got to her door, he didn't hesitate to unlock the door and enter. He just wanted to get in and get out.

Flicking on the light switch right by the entrance, Jordan looked around. The first thing he noticed was how clean and neat everything was. Nothing was out of place, and it looked like a model apartment they showed to get a person to sign a lease. He went through a few of her cabinets in the kitchen and peered into her hallway bathroom, but nothing jumped out to him as suspicious.

The closet, he remembered.

He moved in the direction of the master bedroom and turned on a lamp inside of it once there. Lia's bed was perfectly made, and he sat down on it for a moment, facing the closet door. He felt ridiculous being in her house spying on her like she was some criminal. His eyes were glued to the silver doorknob, and he had an inward battle with himself about whether he was going to look inside. He almost said forget it and walked out the way that he came. Almost.

I'm already here.

He figured he'd rather see for himself that he was tripping instead of wondering about it later. Standing, he took a few steps on the soft carpet and opened the closet door. It was dark inside, and he noticed that most of her clothes were gone, because they were at his house. He felt around the walls of the walk-in closet until he found the light switch. The moment the lights came on, he wished they hadn't. What he was looking at in her closet was something that he didn't understand.

"What the . . ."

He moved closer to the far back wall and moved the few articles of clothing that were in the way so that he could get a better look.

"'My girl'?" He read out loud.

In front of him was an entire wall dedicated to Matise. There were multiple pictures of her. Some of them looked as if Matise didn't even know they were being taken. In one, she was out having breakfast with her friend Amara in New York. And in another, she was sleeping in her bed at home. Jordan knew those fluffy yellow pillows because he and Matise often video chatted before bed. He held his hand out to the wall and touched some of the notes surrounding the pictures.

"'Phrases to learn,'" Jordan kept reading. "'Character traits'?"

The more he read, the worse the queasy feeling in his stomach got. He didn't want to believe what he was seeing. He couldn't believe it. Had Lia studied his best friend to get close to him? If so, that meant she was just like the women before her, only after his money. But to go so far as to stalk Matise? Now that was just sick. His eyes fell on a large shoebox on the ground, and he saw that a paper was sticking out of it. He leaned down and took the top off it. Seeing that it wasn't a paper, but papers in a folder, he picked it up and thumbed through it.

"What the fuck?" he whispered.

The top of the folder said two words that gave him chills: "Becoming Matise." As he read the documents, his heart started to race, and his eyes grew as big as saucers. He realized that he had never really known who Lia was. The very first page was a copy of a scheduled surgery, and attached to it was a photo. Not just any photo. It was a picture of Matise's nose, enlarged and clear as day. Lia had scheduled a surgery to take place after the wedding to get her nose reconstructed to be exactly like Matise's. The next page was the confirmation of a different surgery, with a picture of Matise's whole face. Lia was going to get her entire face done to look as close to Matise as she could. She was crazy, and the next pages he read solidified that. Who the hell had he been lying with all this time? How hadn't he seen the signs? At first, he thought it was just a coincidence that Lia acted and sounded so much like Matise. He thought that he'd finally found another woman who understood him in ways that no one else did. Now he knew it was all an act. He was so overcome with feelings of confusion, anger, and betrayal that he dropped the papers, backed out of the closet, and closed the door.

The moment he stepped back into the room, he heard the front door open and slam shut. He was so stunned by all the information swarming in his head that he didn't move, even when he heard footsteps headed toward him.

"Who's there? Who the hell is in my house?"

It was Lia. When she finally got to the bedroom and saw him standing there, the shocked expression that washed over her face was priceless. She looked around the room first, as if to see if anything was out of place, before looking back at him.

"Jordan, what are you doing here?"

Jordan just stared at her without saying a word. He couldn't even look at her the same. When he didn't say anything, Lia kept talking to him like things were normal.

"After you dropped me off, I noticed that my keys were missing, and I thought I must have lost them or somebody stole them. I had to use the spare keys I keep in my Chanel bag to rush over here to make sure nobody had broken in. But it's just you. Why are you here?" She tried to take a step toward him, but he quickly moved back, and that caused her eyebrows to shoot up. "Jordan, what's wrong?"

"Who the hell are you?" he finally asked.

"What do you mean who am I? I'm Lia," she said and put her arms up.

"Is that even your real name?" he asked.

She furrowed her brow and shook her head slightly as if she didn't understand why he was acting like that. His eyes flickered to the closet, and so did hers. She could see from the little space under the door that the light was on, and Jordan heard her take a sharp breath.

She put her hands up in front of her chest and tried to move toward him again. "Jordan, I can explain."

"You know, when I got this message tonight telling me that you aren't who you say and to come look inside your closet, I thought I was crazy for actually doing it. I thought I was losing my mind, and if you found out, I didn't know how I would explain it to you. But now, I don't think there is any kind of explanation for the sick shit I saw in there."

"Jordan. Jordan, please," she begged. "It's not what it looks like."

"Are you sure? Because it looks like you're trying to steal Matise's identity," he said, and when she tried to touch him, he snatched away violently. "Stay the hell away from me! Don't touch me. Don't ever touch me again. How did you get those pictures of her sleeping, Lia? Were you in her house? This shit is too crazy for me. It's over. Something is fucking wrong with you."

"Jordan, please don't leave me," she sobbed with tears running down the sides of her face. "You're all I have. Please."

"The wedding is off, and I will have all of your things mailed to you. Stay away from me, my family, and Matise!

And you're fired! If I or anyone else catches you on the company's premises, I will have you locked up. The same goes for my home. You need to be in somebody's nut house."

"Jordan, wait!"

She lunged for him and held on to his arm when he tried to walk past her toward the door. He tried to tug away, but she had a strong grip on him. They tussled around the room for a while, and whenever Jordan thought he'd gotten free, she would grab hold of another part of his body. She breathed heavily like a wild animal, and the expression on her face was that of a crazed woman.

"You're not leaving me! You're never leaving me! Do you understand me?" she said with her face pressed against his cheek.

She then proceeded to climb on him to get him to the ground and pin him down. For a woman, she had a lot of strength in her little body. He had no choice. Jordan had never laid a hand on a woman in his life, but he slapped Lia so hard that her neck snapped to one side. The power of the blow forced her to let him go, and she lost her balance. As she was falling into the wall behind her, Jordan hightailed it out of there and dropped her set of keys on the ground on the way out. As the front door slammed behind him, he heard her let out a scream like a banshee's.

"Jordannnn!"

When he got in his car, he made mental notes to up the security on his home and his job. He never wanted to see Lia again.

Chapter 17

Lia

Lia lay on the floor of her bedroom for two days with only a blanket wrapped around her. She hadn't eaten, and she'd barely slept a wink. She couldn't believe that Jordan had left her, and all of the hopes of becoming Mrs. Jordan Heart went out the door with him. Her entire world had crumbled at her feet, and that caused her to sink into a major depression. It felt as though she had cried out all the water in her body, and she just lay there with puffy eyes, staring at the wall. Her hair was disheveled, and the right side of her face still felt like it stung. Jordan had hit her, but she knew he didn't mean it.

"He didn't mean it. He didn't mean it. He didn't mean it," she said, curling up into a fetal position. She pulled her knees to her chest. "He's going to be back, Yeah. He'll be back. He has to come back. Yeah, he has to come back. He loves me."

"You need to be in somebody's nut house!"

His voice echoed over and over loudly in her head, and she slammed her hands on her ears to stop it, but it only got louder. "No, I don't!" she called out. "I won't go!"

Jordan's voice soon turned into her father's, and Lia clenched her eyes shut, attempting to block it all out.

"I don't want to leave. Mommy, please don't let him make me go," she whimpered as the memories began to swarm around her. "Please, Mommy. Please."

"She needs help, LeeAnn!"

Sixteen-year-old Malia Trenton sat at the bottom of the stairwell, listening as her parents did what they did every night: argue about what to do about her. She'd been seeing a psychiatrist three days a week for the past six months, but nothing helped. Malia had a temper that frightened almost everyone around her. When she was sweet, she was an angel. But when she was mad, she was the devil himself. Her latest stunt happened earlier that day. She'd put ammonia mixed with bleach inside of the girls' basketball team's water tank. It hadn't been proven that it was her, but her parents knew it was.

The varsity captain, Ashley Lunes, had recently kicked Malia off the team because she saw her boyfriend flirting with Malia at lunchtime. She lied to the coach and told him that Malia had been in their locker room having sex with some boy. Malia tried to tell the coach that it wasn't true, but the rest of the team backed up Ashley's lie. For that, they all had to pay. Ashley and a few other girls who drank from the tank had all been hospitalized immediately. They would live, but they would know never to mess with Malia again.

"She's seeing her therapist regularly!" LeeAnn spoke quickly. *"I don't think she was the one to do it, honey."*

"Oh, come on! Don't be stupid. Look around! Something is wrong with that girl, LeeAnn! She needs to be in somebody's nut house! Next time she's really going to kill someone. Do you want that blood on your hands?"

"I'm not sending my baby away to be around a bunch of crazies."

"What do you think she is?"

"She's not crazy! And she's your daughter."

"You're in denial. Who do you think put that bleach in our bath soap? That happened right after we told her that she couldn't go to the movies. And that time

we noticed those knives missing? We had to sleep with our bedroom door locked and the dresser slid in front of it for weeks! I can't live like this under my own roof anymore. She has to go! The brochure for the facility is right there on the dining room table."

A few seconds went by, and Malia heard papers rustling. Her breathing was shallow, and her heart was beating faster than it ever had before. They wanted to put her in a nut house? Her fists clenched tight, and she wished that she'd been more discreet when she took those knives from the kitchen. She should have taken the sharp ones in the drawer, not the ones in her mother's knife set on the counter.

She got up from the staircase and walked through the foyer of their two-story house and into the dining room, letting them know that she'd been listening to them the whole time. "You want to send me away?" she asked, glaring at them.

It was a little past six in the evening, and her father had just gotten home from work. He was a car mechanic, so he was still in his dirty work clothes. He was six feet tall and had the body of a manly man. His beard connected with his sideburns on his chocolate face, and he kept the hair on his head cut low. When he saw Malia enter, he didn't seem the least bit intimidated, and he matched her glare.

"Want to? No. Need to? Yes," he said without remorse. "You need help, Malia. Help that you can't get here in this house anymore. You are a danger to yourself and those around you."

"Mama?" she asked to see if she agreed.

Her mother was a petite woman with a pretty face, a small waist, and wide hips. She was what people called a Suzy Homemaker, being that she was a stay-at-home wife and mom. She was wearing her favorite pair of jeans and a state T-shirt she'd gotten when she went to Georgia the year before. Her thick black hair was pulled up into a roll, and her eyes, the same ones Malia had, looked worrisomely back at her daughter.

"Malia, it might be for the best," she said meekly.

"Might be?" He looked at LeeAnn like she had said the most preposterous thing he'd ever heard.

"Don!"

"No, LeeAnn, she almost killed five girls!"

"I didn't do it!" Malia exclaimed.

"Yeah," Don scoffed. "Like hell you didn't. Just like you didn't put that bleach in the bath soap. The school officials said there was bleach in the water that those girls drank. Now that's just too much of a coincidence for me!"

That's when Malia did something that put the most frightened expression on her mother's face. She laughed. She began to laugh so eerily that she put a chill in the room. She threw her head back and held her stomach, and when she was done, she looked at both of her parents with evil eyes.

"They deserved it," she said in an even tone. "When people do terrible things to me, bad things happen to them. I heard that they were going to live, though. They must not have drunk enough."

"Oh my God." LeeAnn rushed to Malia, gripped her by the shoulders, and began to shake her violently. "You don't mean that. Say that you didn't mean that!"

"I can't, because I meant it. I wish all of those whores died," Malia replied in a harsh, flat tone. She wasn't fazed by any of the shaking, and her eyes never left her mother's. "If you send me away, I'm going to kill you."

"That's it!" Don exclaimed and scooped Malia up from off the ground in his strong arms. "She's leaving tomorrow! I already called the facility, and they can have a van here by nine o'clock in the morning."

"You called them without telling me?"

"Stop it, LeeAnn! She isn't your baby anymore. She's a damn psychopath!" Don said as Malia savagely fought against his hold on her. "She has to go."

"Mommy, please don't let him take me," Malia pleaded. Gone was the flat tone, only to be replaced by the whiny voice of a sixteen-year-old girl. It was the same voice she used whenever she was accused of doing something that she said she didn't do. "Please, Mommy! I'll be good! I promise I'll be good."

Malia reached out for her mother, but LeeAnn backed into the wall behind her in fear. LeeAnn placed shaky fingers to her lips as she watched Malia writhe in Don's arms like a creature from hell. Tears slid down her face, and she clutched her chest as she slid down the wall. She sobbed silently and shook her head.

"You're a demon. You aren't my little girl. You have to get out of my house."

"Nooo!" Malia screamed and somehow got free of her father's clutches. "I don't want to leave, Mommy. Please don't let him make me go! Please!"

She lunged at her mother, but her father caught her midair and flung her on his shoulder. She used her fists, nails, and teeth to try to get loose again, but it was no use. She looked up and saw her mother becoming more and more distant as he walked away.

"You aren't my little girl," LeeAnn repeated. "I don't know you. Take her away from me."

"I'm going to kill you! I'm going to kill you!" Malia screamed over and over while her father carried her down the stairs.

He took her to the small, empty room in their basement and set her down. He braced himself to fend her off just in case she tried to attack him again, but she didn't. Instead, she scooted herself into a corner and began to rock with her knees to her chest.

"*You need help, Malia,*" he said in a stern voice. "*Your mother and I have to do what's best for us. You're just not right in the head. Do you know how it feels to know you have a daughter with a sadistic mind? I don't know what you're going to do next.*"

"*I don't want to go,*" Malia whispered.

"*You don't have a choice. I'm calling them back. They'll be here in the morning.*"

She blinked once and looked up at him where he towered over her. "*I said, I don't want to go. And I'm not going. Mommy is going to come get me from down here.*"

"*No, she isn't.*" He smiled sinisterly at her. "*Who do you think helped me install the new lock?*"

Her eyes flickered to the new golden lock, and her eyes widened for a split second. No, it couldn't be true. Not her mother. Don chuckled as the realization spread on her face.

"*I never wanted a kid, especially not one as screwed up as you. But now, we're going to be free to live our lives. Without you.*"

He looked disgustedly down at Malia, like she was a slug, and shut the door. She heard a clicking sound and knew that he had locked it from the outside. The first time that he locked her down there was when she was younger and killed their pet cat by hanging it from the living room fan with a belt around its neck. He didn't know what to do with her, so he put her in the basement until LeeAnn came home. After that, he would lock her down there whenever the two of them were alone together. He would never admit it, but he was terrified of what his own daughter might do when his back was turned. So instead of watching over his shoulder, he would just lock her up.

Up until that day she didn't think her mother knew about what The Room was used for. Malia would never have done anything to hurt LeeAnn. The bleach and the knives had always been for her father. He never liked her, even before she killed the cat. She knew it. She felt it. He was always mean to her and always telling her no. Now there he was, trying to ship her off. Malia always thought that her mom was on her side and one day, after she killed her father, the two of them could leave and go somewhere far, far away. But she knew. She knew the whole time that her husband locked her daughter up alone for hours, and for that, she had to suffer too.

Don was so sure that the room was foolproof and there was no way that Malia could leave it. He'd gone through extra lengths to make sure that she couldn't get out even if she tried. He'd even put a window bar on the outside of her window just in case she thought of escaping. Little did he know, she was three steps ahead of him.

Ashley Lunes thought that her boyfriend had been flirting with her, and he kind of was. Everyone knew that Gerron McClain's father owned a well-known furniture and hardware store called Home Right there in Texas. He had learned a few skills from his old man and promised to help her get free the next time her dad locked her up in exchange for her virginity. She agreed, although she had no intention of following through on that promise. At the same time as the girls' basketball game that night, Gerron snuck over to Malia's house and loosened the window grill so that all she had to do was push it and climb out.

Malia waited for hours before she made her move. She listened until she didn't hear any more footsteps above her head, and then she stood. Opening the window and removing the screen was the easy part, but the window grill was heavy, and she had to put her back into it when she was pushing it. After a few pushes, it fell with a small thud in the grass next to their cement patio in the backyard. She wasted no time in hoisting herself up and out of that cold room.

Not wanting the neighbors to see someone running around the yard in the dark, she walked around to the front of the house. Sinister thoughts plagued her mind as she unlocked the front door with the spare key her mother kept in the flowerpot. She opened the door quietly, and just like she suspected, the alarm wasn't on. Her parents always forgot to turn it on before they went to sleep. Coming from upstairs were the light snores from her father and the faint smell of cigarette smoke. LeeAnn only smoked when she was stressed out, and it had been one of those nights for her.

Malia tiptoed up the wooden stairs, being sure to skip over the ones that squeaked, and went directly to the entrance of their room. Their television gave the only light in the hallway, and when Malia peeked inside, she expected to see LeeAnn awake watching it. When Malia saw that they were both asleep, she waited for a second to make sure they wouldn't stir before entering.

She surveyed them from the end of their bed and noticed that her mother had fallen asleep with a lit cigarette in her hand. Her arm was hanging off the edge of the bed, and the cigarette was lodged between her fingers. Malia also saw the half-empty bottle of vodka on the nightstand next to her father's bed. She was sure that if she got close enough then, she would be able to smell the liquor on his breath.

"Tsk, tsk, Mommy. Don't you know that could cause a fire?" she asked in a whisper. "And, Daddy, don't you know a drunk isn't worth a damn thing?"

The wicked smile spread across her face when she noticed that LeeAnn's cigarette was going out. Malia approached her mother's side of the bed and leaned down to the point where their identical noses were almost touching. She smelled vodka, and it shocked her. LeeAnn never drank, not even during social gatherings. Malia must have driven her off an edge, and instead of feeling sympathetic, Malia got even angrier. Her mother's mind had been poisoned by the same man who treated her only daughter like a criminal. There was no fixing that corruption, and Malia was at peace with what she was about to do. She kissed LeeAnn lightly on her forehead.

"I love you, Mommy. Here, let me help you out," she whispered, picking up the lighter that was lying beside LeeAnn's pillow. She relit the cigarette she was holding. Instead of leaving her arm hanging off the bed, Malia carefully lifted it and rested her hand on the black comforter. "There you go."

She backed away slowly from her parents until she was back at the entrance of the door. It happened quicker than she thought. At first, the cigarette just burned a hole in the cover, but then she saw the first flame. And then she saw the second. Malia didn't leave the room until the bottom of the bed was covered in flames, and the best part was neither of her parents woke up to scream. Their wish was to be without her, and she granted them that. Turned around she went to the stairs and skipped down them, smiling as the fire grew bigger and bigger behind her.

Lia shook her head wildly to push the memory to the way back of her head. The only time she thought about her parents was when she didn't take her medication, and it had been two days since she'd done so. After she and Isaiah took care of his parents, Isaiah helped her get the help she needed. She let him schedule her an appointment with a doctor who prescribed her medications that didn't quite rid her of her anger entirely, but they aided her in controlling it. She trusted Isaiah back then because he had been the only person to ever care about her, but that was the past.

There was only one person who would have sent Jordan that message. There was only one other person who knew the location of her apartment to give him a hint like that about her. And that was Isaiah. For his own gain, he'd taken away the only form of merriment that she'd ever come close to having. He would probably tell her that he was protecting her from being hurt because he loved her. But that was not love. That was betrayal. And when people crossed her, they suffered the ultimate price.

Chapter 18

Lia

I'm so in love with you
Whatever you want to do
Is all right with me

Jacob and Cynthia Heart danced in the enormous basement of their home together, singing along with Al Green. Their feet glided along the red carpet, and they did circles around the pool table and all their furniture. Jacob wore a wine-colored suit with diamond cuff links, and Cynthia wore a black diamond-studded dress. Anyone else would have assumed that they were going out to have a night on the town, but they weren't. They were going to enjoy their own company inside the comforts of their own home. It was a very special night for them, and they were all smiles. They were celebrating that their son had single-handedly gotten J-Net out of a hole that had caused Jacob many sleepless nights.

"I don't know how he did it, and I don't care," Jacob's voice boomed. "I'd trust him with my life!"

"Oh, I know you would, honey!" Cynthia said to her husband and kissed him on the lips. "I'm just glad he was able to snap back into business mode so soon after breaking things off with Lia. Did he ever tell you why they called the wedding off?"

"Just that he realized before it was too late that she wasn't the girl for him."

"Mmm, you know our son has always been a pretty good judge of character. And you know what else?"

"What's that?"

"I always wanted Matise to be my daughter-in-law anyways."

"Oh, you stop it," Jacob laughed. "Now you know if those two wanted to be together they would have been by now."

"I don't know." Cynthia gave her husband a knowing look. "That boy went and found the closest thing to Matise, and he probably figured out that she was the knock-off version. You know he flew out to New York this morning, right? I bet you he realized what he really wants. And if that's the case, I'm all for it."

"Well you know I'm for whatever you're for," he said and nibbled on her neckline.

"Now you stop it, you devil you," she giggled.

"I don't see you making me stop," he growled down at her. "I think that rosé went straight to a certain part of my body, if you know what I mean."

He slid his hands down her back and squeezed her bottom with his large hands. She giggled again, and the older couple shared a passionate kiss. It was obvious that after all those years, the love they had between them was still going strong.

"I think it's getting to me too," she said and gazed up at him with longing eyes. "Do you hear that?"

"Hear what?"

"That voice telling me to go upstairs and take all of my clothes off."

"Oh, *that* voice. Yeah, baby. I hear it loud and clear. Go on, I'll be up in a second," he said and slapped her on the bottom when she turned to walk away. "I don't want you in anything but your birthday suit when I come upstairs, you hear me, woman?"

"Yes, big daddy." She winked back at him when she reached the stairs. "Don't keep me waiting too long now."

"I won't," he assured her.

When she was all the way upstairs, he went to the bar and poured himself another glass of wine. Instead of drinking it right away, however, he placed it on the cream-colored bar countertop and disappeared into one of the back rooms. When he returned, there was a blue pill in his hand, and he took it with a bottled water he got out of the minifridge behind the bar. Just as he was about to grab his glass of wine, he heard a rustle of noise behind him. He whipped around with an eyebrow raised.

"Cynthia, honey, is that you?" he asked, but no answer came. "Hello, who's there?"

Little did he know, there was a set of eyes watching his every move. Lia had been waiting like a cheetah in the jungle for the perfect time to pounce. All day she and Cynthia had been alone. Cynthia didn't know that though. The sad thing about black people was that when they moved out of the hood and into those white neighborhoods, they got careless. Cynthia never even heard Lia enter the home through the side patio door.

The original plan had been to attack him in his sleep, but when she heard Cynthia talking on the phone earlier in the day, plans changed. She said that she and Jacob would be enjoying an intimate night at home together. Lia recalled Jordan telling her that his father had let him know in confidence that he was having some trouble getting it up in the bedroom. Because of that, he had been using Viagra, which he kept hidden in the extra bedroom downstairs. Lia knew one way or another he would have to come downstairs, so that's where she hid. In the furnace room for hours, she peered out of the vents in the door. At first, Lia didn't have a reason to harm Jordan's mother, but now hearing what she had to say, she was beginning to change her mind. She would make that decision later.

She liked watching Jacob's uncertain face. She'd made the noise on purpose, to let him know that he was not alone. She wanted to watch him squirm uncomfortably, but when his eyes fell on the door she was hiding behind, the fun in that was over too soon. His gaze found hers, and he took a step back.

"W . . . who's there? Who are you?"

She knew the jig was up, and she opened the door wide enough for her to walk out of it. She was wearing black formfitting pants, a black hoodie, and black peep-toe booties, and her hair was in two tight buns on the top of her head. The look of fear left Jacob's face only to be replaced with one of confusion.

"Lia? What are you doing in my house?"

"I came to have a little talk with you," she said, walking slowly toward him but stopping to sit on top of the pool table. "If you don't mind."

"Don't mind? You need to leave my house immediately before I call the police and report a break-in."

"I actually didn't break in." Lia made a face and shrugged one of her shoulders. "Your wife didn't lock the side door this morning."

"Morning? You've been in my house since this morning?"

"That's not important," Lia said and chuckled. "What's important is that we need to talk about your son."

"Now, Lia. I understand that you may be having some feelings of anger toward Jordan for breaking things off with you. But you have to let it go and move on with your life. You can't force someone to be with you, and there isn't a thing that I can say to him once his mind is made up. I'm sorry he fired you, and I'll be more than happy to cut you a check to get you by for the rest of the year. There's no reason for you to break into my home looking like some sexy burglar."

"Oh, how sweet of you." Lia put her hand to her heart and pretended to be touched. "But that wasn't the son I was speaking of."

Jacob's face dropped completely. "I don't know what you're talking about."

"Oh really? So, you didn't father a child thirty years ago?"

"No, I did not," Jacob said and regained his composure.

"Tsk, tsk. I'm going to give you one last chance to tell me the truth, Jacob," Lia said in a tone that one would use with a small child.

"That is the truth. I only have one son. Now *I'm* going to give *you* one last chance to leave peacefully before I call the police."

He was a good liar. That was one secret he must have planned to take to the grave. Too bad it came back to haunt him first. Lia studied him as he calmly grabbed his wine glass and downed the entire thing, making a face as it made its way down his throat.

"Is that what you told Isaiah when he came to your office?"

At the mention of Isaiah's name, the queasy look returned to Jacob's face as he looked at Lia. "Who are you?"

"Oh, I don't know." Lia shrugged and hopped down from the pool table. She kept her tone friendly as she spoke and used her hands for emphasis. "I'm just Isaiah's cousin, on his mom's side obviously, who he hired to infiltrate your business for his own personal gain. See, when he came to visit you in your office and you shunned him, you really pissed him off. You shouldn't have done that. Now you have an angry beast on your hands, one who wants everything that you have. Don't you want to know who helped Jordan get you out of that steep hole? Who on earth could do something so gallant? Why, Isaiah of course!"

"What? No, you're lying. Jordan doesn't even know him!"

"And that's where you're wrong. See, it's actually a really funny story," she chuckled and checked the gold Rolex on her wrist. "The original plan was for Jordan and me to get married, right? And then I would talk him into going into business with Isaiah. We had to keep his nosy little sidekick busy right? So, guess who Isaiah started dating?"

"Matise," Jacob said in disbelief.

"Ding, ding, ding! And I'm sure you recall them coming to spend the weekend with us not too long ago. That's how they met and made a deal between the two companies. Now, do you know why Jordan didn't tell you how he got you out of the hole?"

"No, but I'm sure that you're about to tell me."

"Right you are. He didn't tell you because Isaiah told him not to. And do you know why he told him not to tell you?" That time she didn't wait for him to respond. "If I know my cousin, it's because he planned to kill you!" Lia almost doubled over laughing. "Whew! I'm sorry. That's funny. He's so damn predictable! God. And after he killed you, Jordan would be next. Voilà, the perfectly orchestrated plan." She waved her hands in the air for effect, but Jacob still hadn't comprehended what she said. "I said, 'Voilà, the perfectly orchestrated plan,'" she repeated, but still she got nothing, and she rolled her eyes. "You can't be that stupid. With both of you dead, that would leave him as your only living successor. He would get everything."

"No." Jacob shook his head and finger at the same time.

"Yes." Lia pursed her lips and nodded her head. "It's true. But I have good news for you. What I just told you wasn't the original plan. If you remember what I said, Jordan and I were supposed to get married before Isaiah started improvising. But when he did, he didn't need me anymore, and here's the problem with that. I fell in love with Jordan in real life." She giggled like a schoolgirl. "I fell hard, too. So hard that I can't allow Isaiah to kill him, because Jordan and I are going to be together."

"You're a sick little bitch." Jacob sneered her way. "You will never have my company or my son!"

"Name-calling?" Lia clicked her tongue on her teeth three times. "Now I'm happy I get to take away another one of Isaiah's joyous moments by killing you myself."

"Ha!" he scoffed. "If that's what your ultimate goal was after all of that yapping, I'd like to see you try. You don't even have any weapons. I'll crush your neck with my bare hands for trying to ruin me!"

Without warning, he came at her with his hands outstretched. Lia had no doubt in her mind that if he got a hold of her, he would kill her, but she still didn't budge. In mid-lunge Jacob Heart stopped and fell to the ground, clutching his chest.

Lia checked her watch again and nodded. "Hmm," she said, impressed. "Right on time."

"What did you do to me?" Jacob groaned. "I can't . . . I can't breathe. My chest!"

"That's because you're having a heart attack," Lia told him like it was rocket science. "You see, while you were in the back room getting your dick-hardening medication, I poured a lethal dosage of potassium chloride in your drink. It's untraceable. When they find you, the only thing that will be in your system is the wine and that Viagra that you need so much."

"Bitch," he said right before his body went rigid and he let out his last breath.

"Terrible choice of a last word, but at least you went out in style," she said to his dead body. "I was going to go upstairs and kill your wife too for the nasty things she said about me, but I think finding you like this is going to be punishment enough. Plus, I have to leave. I have a red-eye to catch to New York."

Chapter 19

Matise

I was still a little hurt behind the whole Isaiah thing. However, I was a strong black woman who could get through anything. Or at least that was what I told myself. I'd taken a chance on love only to have it crash and burn right in my face. I thought surely he would try to call me to make up, but that call never came. That led me to believe that he had been playing the field the whole time. It hurt, but if that was the case, then he could have told me from the beginning.

That was the problem with men, they were selfish. They constantly took away our choice to deal with them accordingly. He had me feeling guilty for having feelings for Jordan when he was playing me the whole time. I tried not to wonder how many other women there had been, because it made me feel like a complete fool. Why I would ever think that a man like that would only deal with one woman was beyond me. Maybe because I was a hopeless romantic and always would be.

I'd tried to call Lia and talk to her about the whole situation, but she hadn't returned my calls in a few days. She was probably completely swamped planning the wedding, which I completely understood. I hadn't even thought to try to ring Jordan. I just didn't feel it was appropriate to call him all hours of the day anymore. Instead, I just drowned myself in work to keep my mind busy. I avoided all Amara's questions about what was going on in my life, because it was just something I didn't want to talk about.

I sat at my desk scrolling through a catalog of work cubicles for a new telecommunications company opening in New York. It was a project that had been keeping me busy all day, and I was so engrossed in my work that I didn't even hear anyone step into my office.

"Hi, I'm here to see a Matise Jackson? Do you know where I can find her?"

"That's m—" I averted my eyes from my computer screen to see Jordan standing in my office. "Jordan!"

I stood up with a smile that went from ear to ear. He was looking handsome as ever in a pair of tan trousers and a tucked-in off-white button-up. We embraced, and he returned my smile when he let me go.

"You look beautiful," he told me, taking notice of how I looked in my coral pencil skirt and aqua blue Givenchy ruffle-trimmed silk-chiffon blouse.

"Thank you," I said and pointed to the large aqua clutch to match. "I wanted to be little fancy today. When you look good, you feel good. What are you doing here, sir?"

"I can't pop up on my favorite person in the world now?"

"Yeah, yeah. How long have you been here?"

"Since the morning."

"And you're just now coming to see me? The day is almost over!"

"I know. I've just had a lot on my mind. Speaking of which, you must have something on yours too."

"And what makes you say that?" I asked, sitting back down.

"Because you only say that 'when you look good, you feel good' crap when you don't feel good. Spill it."

I hated how well he knew me sometimes. I rolled my eyes to the ceiling and let out a big breath. I didn't want to talk about it, but sooner or later he was going to find out anyway.

"Isaiah and I aren't dealing with each other anymore," I said to him.

"What? I thought you really liked dude."

"I did. I mean I thought I did. But he wasn't honest with me, and I blew up on him. Now we're not talking."

"That's crazy."

"I know, I know," I said, smacking my lips because I wasn't trying to hear his mouth. "I should have never brought him to meet you or my parents."

"I wasn't going to say that. I was going to say that's crazy because I called off the wedding with Lia."

"Huh?" I heard what he said, but it didn't make any sense. I thought he loved her, or that's what it seemed like. What confused me even more was that he looked just as puzzled as me. He took a seat in one of the two empty chairs on the other side of my desk and placed his elbows on the table.

"She wasn't who she said she was," he told me. "She was . . . obsessed."

"With you?"

"No. With you."

"Come again?"

"She was obsessed with you, Te Te. That's why I'm here. I wanted to tell you that you may need to change your locks. I think . . . I think Lia might have been in your place."

"Wait, wait. I don't get what you're saying. She doesn't know where I live."

"I think she does. She had pictures of you sleeping in your bed and pictures of you and Amara eating. She had all these notes written up about you. She was studying you. She had to have been. That's why she reminded me so much of you. Your phrases, your mannerisms, everything. She even was planning to get surgery to look more like you."

"Jordan, you're scaring me," I said. "Stop playing."

"I'm telling you the truth. I saw the documentation confirming her surgery appointments." He stopped to clench and unclench his jaw before talking again. "That's not all I found."

The worried look in his eyes made me nervous to ask what else he found. His whole countenance was making the hairs on the back of my neck stand at attention. "What did you find?"

"Files."

"What kind of files?"

"They were files from a psych ward, Te Te. Her name isn't Lia Blackstone. It's Malia Trenton. She was admitted a few years back for aggravated assault."

"How did she get out?"

"I didn't read that far," Jordan admitted. "All I know is that she's the worst kind of bad news, and I want you to protect yourself. Get a gun or something. This is all my fault."

"No, don't blame yourself. It's my fault too. I should have noticed the signs. I hated to admit it, but she was a lot like me. I guess that's why she grew on me." I spun in my chair and held my stomach in hopes of keeping my lunch down. "Oh boy. This is . . . Wow."

"She's been blowing my phone up so much I had to turn it off."

"What are you going to do?"

"I don't know," Jordan said, rubbing his hands down his face. "Hope she leaves me alone I guess. Has she tried to contact you?"

"No. I haven't talked to her since—" My eyes grew as wide as saucers. "She's the reason why Isaiah and I are done talking. She told me he got a girl's number in the club, and . . . Oh my God. She was probably lying."

"Damn."

"I'll have to apologize to him," I said, letting my stomach go. "I was really mean to him."

"Do you think you two will get back to how you used to be?" Jordan asked and gave me a look that I couldn't read.

"With all of this crazy shit going on? I might need a man to protect me, but I honestly don't know. Probably not now."

"Good," Jordan said looking relieved, but then he tried to catch himself.

"Uh-uh." I furrowed my brow at him. "Why did you just say 'good'?"

He didn't answer me right away. Instead, he pushed away from the desk and got to his feet. He started to pace back and forth, which was something he always did when he was nervous, but what could he have been nervous about?

"I've just had a lot of time to think, you know, with the whole Lia thing," he finally said, looking me dead in my eyes. "And she did all of these things to become you, and I fell in love with her."

"Yeeeaah."

"But I didn't really fall in love with *her*, did I?"

"What are you saying, Jordan?" I said, my voice barely over a whisper.

He sighed deeply before he rounded the desk and kneeled in front of me. "I'm saying that I kept thinking about her being close enough to hurt you, and it drove me crazy. I thought at first it was because you're my friend, but it's deeper than that. I felt it in my bones that I had to come to New York to be with you, to protect you, and not just as your friend. That's why it took me so long to come up here, because I was trying to put all this shit in my head into words."

Was what I thought was happening really happening? Jordan took my hands in his and pressed them to his chin, staring at me in a way that he'd never done before. I tried to catch my breath, but I couldn't. It was like every emotion for him that I thought had left my system came back all at once.

"Jordan, I think you might just be a little shocked with everything going on with Lia," I whispered. "The crazy stuff she did might have you a little confused about the way you feel."

"No, I was confused before. Not anymore."

"Jordan, please, you're just—"

"Tell me something, Te Te."

"What?"

"The night of our college graduation, when I asked who you thought my perfect girl was, who did you describe?"

"Jordan, stop."

"When you said you had something to tell me, you were going to tell me that you loved me, weren't you?"

I didn't have to answer with words because the tears in the corners of my eyes spoke loudly enough.

"I knew what you wanted to tell me," he continued and placed his palm on my cheek. "I knew you loved me, and I knew why you hated every single girl I dated, so I shut it down before you could say it."

"Why?"

"Because I loved you too," he said and kissed my hand. "I loved you too much to hurt you. You are the most precious part of my life, and I wanted to keep you in it as long as I could. I wasn't an ounce of shit back then. After you moved away, I tried to find pieces of you in other women, but I was never satisfied."

"Until you met Lia." I shook my head. "I don't want to be your rebound, Jordan."

"Rebound? You were always the first shot, and my biggest regret will always be that it took a fake to help me see that. Matise?"

He put both of his hands on my thighs, forcing them apart so that he could move closer to me. I didn't push him off me when he pressed his torso all the way to my panty line. I also didn't stop him when he put his muscular arms around my waist. In fact, I shivered.

"Yes?" I breathed.

"Do you still love me?"

"Yes," I admitted. "That's why I didn't want you to get married."

"I'm sorry for putting you through that. Matise?"

"Yes?"

"I love you too."

His lips found mine, and for a second I wrapped my arms around his shoulders and kissed him back. Okay, it was more like five minutes. I had wondered for years what his kisses would feel like, and amazing wasn't even the word to describe them. His lips were even softer than I ever imagined, and our tongues danced together like long-lost friends. I pulled away abruptly and put my hands on his chest to stop him from leaning in again. I felt lightheaded. He'd given me too much information, and it was all racing through my mind and giving me an overwhelming feeling.

"What's wrong?"

"It's just a lot," I told him. "I love you, Jordan, I really do. But there is so much that we need to think about. I just got out of a situation with Isaiah because of something that might not even be true. With what you told me about Lia, I don't know if I can go home. And now you're telling me that you love me. It's just too much for me right now."

"I understand." Jordan nodded, but I could tell that he was disappointed. "Maybe you should go stay with your assistant for a while if you can. And about Isaiah—"

"Jordan—"

"He'll have to kill me before I let him have you. Now that I know what I want, I'm not going to let you go. So, if you need to go and get your closure with that situation, be my guest. But I'm not going anywhere. I'll be staying at the Manx Palace if you don't want to go home tonight."

He kissed me one last time on my cheek, stood up, and left the way he came. Stunned wasn't the word to explain what I was feeling. I fixed my skirt and scooted my chair back up to my desk so that I could try to get back to work. I should have known that would be a no-go. I couldn't concentrate to save my life.

Knock! Knock!

"Was that Jordan I just saw walking up out of here?" Amara asked, as usual barging in without waiting for me to tell her she could enter. That day she was wearing a plum-colored maxi dress that went all the way down to the floor. Her hair was in two Cherokee braids, and she batted her long eyelash extensions at me.

"Yeah." I cleared my throat. "He, um, came to tell me some things. How didn't you know that he was here if he had to walk by your desk?"

"I had to take a late lunch today. I'm sorry, boss lady," she said, responding in a way that made me sure she noticed my condescending tone.

"I'm sorry, I don't mean to sound irritable. I just have a lot of things on my mind."

"I bet. Well, let me know if you need anything."

"Okay," I said, but then stopped her before she was all the way out of the door. "Amara? I do need something."

"What's up?"

"Do you think I could stay at your place for a few days? Not tonight, but maybe tomorrow and a few days after?"

"You know I don't care, girl. I have a second bedroom that's fully furnished with nobody to use it. Is everything okay?"

"Yeah," I lied. "I just don't want to be at home, that's all."

"I understand." Amara looked at me sympathetically. "You're always welcome to stay anytime."

"Thanks, girl," I said, and she flashed me a smile before she went back to her desk.

The more I thought about the situation with Lia, the more frightened I became. I believed every word that Jordan had told me. I could see it in his eyes that he was telling the truth. He wasn't the kind of person who would want to scare me on purpose, so his warning was one that I was heeding. I'd told Amara that I wouldn't be staying at her place that night because the wind would most likely blow me to Jordan's hotel. But not before I went and had a chat with Isaiah.

Chapter 20

Isaiah

It hadn't happened the way that he originally wanted it to. In fact, things had turned out to be better than Isaiah expected. Every loose end had been cut off, and whereas he had not acquired J-Net, he got something much better. Affiliation. Now that J-Net and NYC Partners were aligned, when Isaiah exacted his ultimate revenge and rid the world of Jordan and Jacob Heart, no one would question his takeover. They would assume that Jacob must have known that Isaiah was his son, and he would be the sole heir to the empire. In all honesty, it had never been about the company. It was about the fact that Jacob had let his firstborn son take the last name of another man. And for that, he would take everything that should have been his.

Isaiah sat cozily in his living room, enjoying a cold beer and catching up on shows that he hadn't had much time to watch in all his scheming and plotting. He hadn't talked to Lia, but that was normal after he paid her for a job. She would go on her merry way, and he would see her again when she needed more money or a refill on her medication. She hadn't called him, and he hadn't called her, and he hoped she wasn't too heartbroken over Jordan. It was for the best, and he was sure she understood that by then.

The one person he did want to call was one of those loose ends that he'd mentioned. He fought the urge to pick up the phone every day and reach out to her, but that wouldn't do anything but hurt them both. Even so, moving on from her was proving to be quite a task. She'd become a part of his everyday life even when he wasn't with her. He missed the way her nose crinkled at its tip when she laughed, and the way she would lie on his chest without moving after a night of making love. Still, there was just too much damage between them, and letting her go was a small price to pay to have everything that he ever wanted. It only took twenty-one days to break a habit, and Matise would soon just be a thing of the past.

He pushed her pretty face to the furthest part of his mind and focused his attention back on the television. He didn't budge from that couch until he drank the rest of his beer and got up to get another one. Once inside the kitchen, he strained his neck so that he wouldn't miss seeing Dean Winchester kick a demon's ass. He turned away only to open the door of his tall, stainless-steel refrigerator, bending down to reach the last beer in the back of it. When he stood back up, Isaiah shut the door and jumped when he saw Lia planted there holding a crowbar in her hand.

"Hey, cousin. Happy to see me?" she asked cheerily.

Before he could do anything, she swung the crowbar once, striking him in his temple, and everything went black.

Chapter 21

Lia

She thought he would wake up on his own, and when he didn't, Lia took it upon herself to bring him back to reality. She tossed a large cup of freezing water on Isaiah, and he jumped to attention. He broke into a fit of coughs and began to gasp for air.

"Stop being dramatic. I was going to use boiling hot water," she said. "But you're my cousin. I wouldn't do that to you."

Isaiah blinked his eyes rapidly and tried to focus on the room around him. He had a stream of blood running down his face, and it had spread to his clothes thanks to the water she'd thrown. It didn't take him long to realize that he was bound to one of his own wooden dining room chairs, and he fought against his restraints. It was no use though. Lia had made it so not even the strongest man in the world could break free of those binds. She sat in a chair directly in front of his, wearing all black and watching him continue to try to detach himself from his seat.

"You're not going to break those knots," Lia told him. "I've gotten pretty good at making them."

"Where am I?" he panted.

"You don't recognize your own house?" Lia sniggered. "All I did was move your couch out of the way to make room for the extracurricular activities this evening. We're going to have some fun."

"Why are you doing this, Lia?" Isaiah asked, still out of breath. "Let me go."

She felt a flicker of anguish, but she let it subside. His ignorance irritated her. A slow smile spread across her glossed-up lips, and she batted her eyelashes at him.

"You mean to tell me that you don't remember what you did?"

"Whatever it is, we can talk about it. Just let me go, please."

"I already gave you a chance to talk about it with me, and you didn't want to. Instead, you took matters into your own hands, didn't you? I was happy, Isaiah. Happy. Do you know how long I've waited to feel that? Do you know how long I've waited to have a solid place to call home? My entire life, that's how long. But noooo, you just had to wreck it for me, just so you could get what you wanted."

"Lia, I didn't do anything. You're being delusional right now," Isaiah said, evening out his tone to a soothing one. "Untie me so we can work through all of this."

"Delusional, huh? Maybe, but I find it funny how Jordan ended up at my apartment and knew exactly where to look to find information about me. I know you sent that text, Isaiah. I know you told Jordan to go into my closet. You were the only other person who knew where I stayed."

"You don't know what you're talking about, Lia. You need to take your medicine."

"And," Lia continued, ignoring him entirely, "I was wondering how you even knew what was there, but then it hit me like a bag of bricks. It almost slipped my mind, but I remembered that Matise told me you disappeared for a while that night we all went out. You went to my house, didn't you?"

"Lia—"

"Didn't you?" Her scream was so loud that he shut up instantly. "And stop using that fucking shrink voice when you talk to me. Goodness, be a man!"

"Fine," Isaiah said and turned his nose up. "I sent the message. I told you to cut him off, and you didn't listen."

"'I told you to cut him off, and you didn't listen,'" Lia mocked him. "That's your problem, Isaiah. You're always trying to be in control of somebody."

"I saved your life." He glared at her.

"And I made you rich." She flared her nose and spoke through her bared teeth. "Don't you ever forget that you would have never gotten your little jumpstart if it weren't for me. You know, I was going to blackmail you and take your company from right under your feet, but I changed my mind. That sounds like something you would do, and I'm so much better than you."

"Only because I'm tied up."

"Even when you aren't," Lia said with her sweet voice. "I have always been able to figure out your next move before you even make it."

"Oh, yeah, like what?" he tried her.

She stood up and leaned toward him until she could place her lips by his ear. "I know Jacob Heart is your father, and I know all you wanted was your daddy's acceptance," she said and then sat back down. The disturbed look that swept over his face made her happy. "But you didn't get that, did you? He made you get out of his office, huh?"

"How do you know all of this?"

"Did you forget that my first original cover was as a secretary at J-Net? When I first started, one of the first jobs I was given was to log all the current and previous month's sign-ins into the computer. Imagine my shock when I saw your name, cousin. All it took to find out the truth was for me to call in a few favors to the friends I had in higher places. But even when I found that out, I didn't change up on you. I stayed loyal to the mission and to you, but then you betrayed me."

"You can't be with Jordan!" he shouted in her face.

"I can, and I will!" she bellowed back like a beast.

"The mission is over, Lia. We got what we wanted already."

"No, you got what you wanted." She shook her head. "Not all of us are as selfish as you, Isaiah. Some of us need more than just money in life. I'm glad Matise dropped your ass. She would be disappointed to know that this is the real you."

"Leave her out of this."

"Ooh, did I strike a nerve? Well, let me strike another one. You must really think I'm dumb, don't you?"

"No."

"I'm going to ask you that question again," she said, putting her right hand into the pocket of her hoodie. She pulled out a pistol and stood up. "This time, be honest. Do you think I'm dumb, Isaiah?"

"No! I don't think you're dumb, Lia."

"Wrong answer!" she yelled and swung the butt of the gun down on his jaw.

The blow knocked his head to the side and drew blood from his mouth. She did it again and again until she was out of breath.

"You do think I'm dumb and incompetent. If you didn't, you wouldn't have just said things like 'the mission is over' and 'we got what we wanted.' You don't think I know what your ultimate scheme was? You wanted Jacob dead, and even more so you want Jordan dead. That's the real reason you don't want me to be with him, because you want to kill him."

"Yes," Isaiah said and weakly brought his head back up to face her. "He has to die."

"You aren't going to lay a hand on him."

"What can you do with him now? Did you not hear what I told you before? He doesn't love you. He loves the person you were trying to be! And now that he knows about all the skeletons you hid in your closet, he'll never forgive you."

"Shut up!" Lia yelled and tried to plug her ears with the gun still in her hand. "Just shut up!"

"You know it's true," he said, reverting to his soothing tone. "All he's going to do is hurt you just like everyone else in your life. I'm the only one who has never hurt you, remember? Just release me so that I can be sure to finish the job, and we can make sure that he never hurts you."

"Finish the job?" she asked, and her mouth spread into a deranged grin. "The job is already finished."

"It's not, because I'm still tied to this chair."

"Do you remember the first plan, cousin? The one where we made sure that Jordan gets the company? Well, he has the company now. He just doesn't know it."

"What the hell are you talking about?"

"Jacob's dead," she said, laughing. "Jacob is dead because I killed him last night. And you will never get the chance to ever lay a hand on Jordan. You will never win. Ever."

"You what?" Isaiah looked furiously at her. "You what?"

He tried his best to get to her, and the chair he was in rocked, making the legs bang on the ground. He screamed curses at her and said many things that might have hurt her feelings if she had her medication in her system. But she didn't, so there was no getting through to her.

"Are you done? Because I have a happily ever after to complete. I just have one more person to get out of the way after you."

She held the gun up to his head, but just as she was about to apply pressure and blow his brains out, the doorbell rang. She gave Isaiah a look that warned him to stay quiet, and she waited for whoever was at the door to go away. Suddenly, she heard the front door to the house open and remembered that she hadn't locked the door after she broke in.

"Isaiah!" a familiar voice called. "Isaiah? I wanted to talk to you. Are you here? Your door was unlocked and I . . . Oh my God!"

Lia smiled, not believing her luck. It was just the person she wanted to see.

"Welcome to the party, Matise."

Chapter 22

Matise

I didn't know what I had just walked into. I had found Isaiah all right, but that came with more than what I bargained for. He was tied up to a chair with his blood all over the place, and Lia was standing in front of him, looking like a hit girl holding a gun. I tried to turn and run away, but Lia held the firearm up and aimed it at me.

"Ah, ah, ah. Leaving so soon?" she taunted. "Sit!"

"Lia. What's going on?"

"I said sit!" she screamed like a lunatic and cocked the gun.

I had no choice but to do what she told me to, and I sat in the chair across from Isaiah. He avoided my eyes as Lia stripped me of car keys and my cell phone. I was perplexed by what was happening because I didn't understand why Lia was at his home in the first place.

"Aw, how sweet. The lovebirds are reunited. So cute," Lia said and made kissy noises. "You look confused, Te Te." She turned to Isaiah and tapped his shoulder with the gun. "Psst! You want to tell her what's going on? No? Okay, I'll tell her."

"Tell me what?" I asked, looking from her to him.

"Isaiah and I are cousins. We do this thing where he calls me to help him blackmail other corporations or invade his competitor's companies for information. This whole thing was a setup. Me and Jordan. Isaiah and you.

Except I really love Jordan, and Isaiah, well, you were disposable to him."

"You're lying. I know who you really are, Malia Trenton." Her eyes flickered when I said her real name. "Jordan told me all about you and how you were in a psych ward. I don't know why they let you out."

"Keep talking and I'm going to do you exactly like I did Jacob Heart before I left Nebraska."

Her words caught me by surprise. She was going to do me like she did Mr. Heart? What had she done to him? "Where is Mr. Heart?"

"Dead on his basement floor," Lia answered with zero remorse. "That is unless his wife found him."

"I don't believe you," I said.

"Tell her, Isaiah. Tell her that everything that I'm saying is true. Tell her that the only reason you were fucking her was to keep her busy in New York while I was in Nebraska with Jordan. Let her know that you're Jacob's bastard son and you were going to kill him and Jordan to take everything from them. Tell her!"

I looked at Isaiah, hoping that Lia had dived off the deep end. Mr. Heart couldn't be dead. She and Isaiah couldn't be cousins. How could he be related to someone so insane?

"Is it true?" I whispered.

"I'm sorry," Isaiah said feebly, confirming Lia's words. "I never meant for you to get hurt in any of this."

"So, Jacob is really your father, and Jordan is your . . . your . . ."

"My brother. Yes," he answered and briskly sucked in air between his teeth. "You don't know how it felt growing up knowing that your own father chose not to be a part of your life. He knew it was a possibility that I was his, and he never investigated it. I had to work hard for everything! So, when I was presented with an opportunity to reimburse myself for all of my sacrifices, I took it."

How had I missed the resemblance? That explained why I had been so attracted to Isaiah in the first place. He and Jordan had the same eyes, and both had gotten their good looks from their father.

"So, everything between us?" I asked, and my voice cracked. "Was it real or fake?"

"A lot of it was real," he sighed and soaked in the hurt I knew he saw in my eyes. "But most of it was fake. I'm sorry, Matise. I was only after one thing, and then you came along."

"Is that why you never called me after I blew up on you?"

"Yes. I wanted to, but there was no point. We could never be together."

It felt as though someone had just gut punched me with an iron fist. I felt my face dropping by the second, and I fell from the chair and onto the floor. I vomited everything I'd eaten that day and didn't stop until all that was left was that nasty green acid. When I was done, Lia grabbed a handful of my hair and yanked me back up into the chair.

"That was repulsive," she said, making a face at me. "I expected you to try to fight him or something, not throw up. You had so much more zest when I first met you. What happened to that firecracker that chewed me out? It's a shame."

"Jordan was right about you. You're crazy," I said through gritted teeth.

"Jordan wouldn't say such things about the woman he loves."

"I know," I said, catching my breath. "He would never say anything like that about me. That's why you want to be like me, isn't it? So he can love you for real? Well, that won't ever happen. You disgust him!"

That must have struck a nerve with her because the next thing I knew, I was seeing stars. I'd never gotten hit with a gun before, and it hurt like hell. She struck me right across my jawline, and I tasted blood instantly.

"He loves me!" she screeched and pistol whipped me again, that time in my temple. "Not you!"

She continued to beat me with the gun until I fell to the ground again. By the time she was done, I couldn't feel my face at all, but I knew it was swelling because I could see my cheeks puffing out. She used her foot to nudge me so that I rolled over to my back, and she pointed the barrel of the gun in my face.

"You made this easy for me," she said. "I thought I was going to have to go find you, but you came right to me. You know, if Isaiah wouldn't have screwed things up, this would never have had to happen. You know you were my girl, right?"

She pulled the trigger, letting off the loudest gunshot ever, just as someone tackled her to the ground. She fell with a loud thud, and the gun fell out of her hand, sliding across the floor. The bullet missed my head by centimeters, and my chest heaved up and down as I silently thanked the heavens. I sat up to see that my savior was Isaiah. Somehow, he'd broken free of his binds and had rammed into Lia in the nick of time.

"Maybe you aren't so good at making binds after all," he said from where he had her pinned down. "You talk too much. I used the time that you were yapping to break free."

He used the rest of his energy to hit her hard enough in the head to knock her out cold. He tried to get up but started to wheeze and fell right back down.

"Isaiah!" I exclaimed and moved my own aching body to help him. "Here, put your arm around my shoulders. Ahhh!"

I shouted out in pain as I helped him to his feet. He'd lost so much blood already that if we didn't get him to the emergency room, and quick, he was going to die. I tried to get him to the front door, but he had to pause and lean against one of the walls.

"I got it," he said and removed his arm from my shoulders. "I'm just weighing you down. Give me two seconds."

I moved in front of him just in case I needed to catch him if he fell. He saw what I was doing and gave me a crooked smile with his swollen lips. "After all that I've done to you, you would still help me?"

"I can't leave you here like this. Come on," I said and tried to force him to walk with me, but he shook his head.

"That's why I never deserved you," he said between his quick breaths. "Matise, I wanted to call you so bad, but—"

"But the things that you need to do to fulfill your life would destroy mine."

"Yes," he said and looked longingly in my eyes. "In a perfect world I would be with you over and over again, but I am just not a man who can love without causing torment. Look at what I did to Lia. She's off her meds and completely has lost it."

"She was already a monster," I told him. "That had nothing to do with you."

"I helped her manifest into an even bigger monster because of my greed. We've done terrible things together. Things that I might wish I could take back."

"Shhh." I shook my head not wanting to hear anymore. I grabbed his arm, and he started to put it back over my shoulder. "Let's get you some medical atten—"

Boom!

The back of Isaiah's head exploded, and his blood splattered everywhere, including on my face. The wall he'd just been leaning on was now covered in pieces of his brain and skull. His eyes were still on me when he dropped to the ground, dead. My mouth was frozen open in a scream, but nothing came out.

"*You* talk too much, cousin. I used the time that *you* were yapping to grab my gun and kill you," Lia said to Isaiah's body before turning back to me with the pistol in her hand. "Now, where were we?"

Chapter 23

Jordan

He had every intention of heading to his hotel, and he did. However, when he got there, he didn't stay there. He couldn't. Not with Matise heavy on his mind the way she was. The feel of her lips lingered on his, and he wanted to feel that again and again. He wanted to hold her and promise that he would protect her from anything that threatened to cause her grief. He'd almost lost her once, and he wasn't going to make that mistake again. And if that meant he had to tell Isaiah to back off, then so be it.

Jordan got Isaiah's home address from the paperwork that had been sent over to him, and he hopped in his rented burnt orange 2017 Dodge Charger. Knowing that Matise had gotten off work already, he hoped that she would come to the hotel and stay the night with him. Even if she did though, knowing her, she was going to stop at home first anyway. Still, he wouldn't want to keep her waiting, so he had to get going.

He pulled out his phone and turned it on after an entire day and hoped that Lia wouldn't start blowing him up again. When everything was up, he shook his head when he saw that he had five voicemails. He assumed that they were from Lia and didn't even bother to click on the voicemail icon. Instead, he opened his navigation app, put in his destination, and drove out of the hotel's parking lot.

He drove in complete silence and tried to figure out what he was going to say to make sure that Isaiah left Matise alone. "This might confuse you since the last time you saw me I was with Lia . . . No." He quickly trashed that and tried again. "Look here, you tall motherfucker, I . . . No."

He needed something that was straight to the point and intimidating, but not so disrespectful to the point that Isaiah backed out on their agreement before the ink dried. He played with a few other sentences on the remainder of the drive there before finally finding the right one.

At last, he reached Isaiah's neighborhood. It was one that put his own little suburb to shame. The houses weren't regular houses. They were mini mansions, and most of them had closed gates around them. When the GPS dinged letting him know that he'd reached the destination, he took notice of the fact that Isaiah's gate was already open. He pulled through and drove on the long, curving driveway until he reached the front of the house. He cleared his throat and practiced his line again in the rearview mirror.

"Look, Isaiah, no hard feelings, but Matise is the woman I love. So, if we are going to be doing business together, I'm going to need for you respect that and step off completely."

He liked how it sounded together, and he liked how he looked, but he needed to add more authority to his voice if he was about to go claim his woman. He took a deep breath and gave himself the most serious look that he could muster.

"Look, Isaiah. You're a cool dude and all, but Matise is the woman I love. If we're going to be doing business together, you need to respect that and back off compl—"

Boom!

Jordan heard the gunshot loud and clear, and it had come from Isaiah's house. He jumped out of the vehicle and slowly approached the door. It was already slightly ajar, and all he had to do was push it for it to open all the way. He almost called out Isaiah's name but thought better of it because he didn't know who all was inside. Most importantly, he didn't know who had the gun.

He treaded lightly as he walked, and the first thing he saw was an aqua blue clutch on the magazine table in the foyer. It looked exactly like the one that Matise had showed him in her office. Jordan opened it up, and sure enough, Matise's driver's license fell out onto the table. His level of concern grew. She must have gone there after she got off work.

He rushed through the foyer of the huge house and went toward the living room. *What if Isaiah killed her? What if she's lying somewhere bleeding? What if she . . .* He stopped thinking crazy thoughts instantly when he got farther into the house. He now knew who had gotten shot. Lying there in a pool of his own blood was Isaiah, and the back of his head had been blown off.

Up ahead he heard someone moving. He left Isaiah where he was. There was nothing left anyone could do for him. He raced to where he heard the noise.

"Matise?" he called out skeptically as he made his way through the living room. He had no idea what had gone on there, but it looked as if someone had been being tortured. Blood was everywhere. "Matise!" he called again when he got to the dining room.

"Jordan!"

He heard her familiar cry and realized that it was coming from outside. Her voice sounded distant, but he ran through the large dining room toward the patio.

"Help, Jordan. She's crazy! It's L—"

He pushed open the glass double doors to the patio. The house had a side driveway that merged with the one in the front. Parked there was a silver 2018 Mercedes-Benz E-Class coupe with tinted windows. He squinted at the car, trying to see through the dark tint, when the engine started.

"Matise?" he called.

The passenger's side window rolled down, and his heart froze over when he became aware that it wasn't Matise in the driver's seat at all. It was Lia.

"If I can't have you, then she can't either!" she yelled out to him.

He then heard the distinctive sound of banging coming from the trunk of the car, and it dawned on him what was happening. Lia gave him one last wicked smile before pressing on the gas with the car in reverse.

"No!" he roared. "Matise!"

He ran as fast as he could after them, but the coupe was faster. Distance easily got put between them, and just in case he thought about following her in his car, Lia shot out the tires on the driver's side as she sped down the driveway and onto the street.

"Matiiiise!" Jordan bellowed in despair one last time.

But it was too late. They were gone.

To be continued